KINDRED SPIRITS

THE HEALERS

KINDRED SPIRITS

THE HEALERS

Rory Church

Black Lyon Publishing, LLC

KINDRED SPIRITS: THE HEALERS
Copyright © 2017 by Keith Zwingelberg

Our books may be ordered through your local bookstore or by
visiting the publisher:

BlackLyonPublishing.com

Black Lyon Publishing, LLC
PO Box 567
Baker City, OR 97814

This is a work of fiction. All of the characters, names, events,
organizations and conversations in this novel are either the products
of the author's vivid imagination or are used in a fictitious way for the
purposes of this story.

ISBN-13: 978-1-934912-76-8
Library of Congress Control Number: 2016956282

Published and printed in
the United States of America.

Black Lyon Romantic Suspense

Dedication

To my mother, Inez Wynne, for embodying me with the drive,
intellect, and inspiration to always reach for perfection.

Acknowledgements

There is an old adage that goes "write what you know." As I have traveled on my
writing journey, several experience authors and teachers have refined that quote
to "know what you write." To obtain that knowledge I have, by necessity, searched
hard to understand the Creek culture and their traditional medicine and sacred
ways. Personally, I would start by thanking Debra Bush of the Lower Muskogee
Creek Tribe of Georgia and Jerry E. Lang, Member Southeastern American Indian
Inter-tribal Elder's Council. I met Debbie and Jerry at a Pow Wow in the Panhandle
of Florida a few years back. At that time I had done extensive book research on the
history, cultural, and medical practices of the Muskogee Creek. Many questions
remained in my mind as to how that heritage had translated to the lives of those
Creek in the twenty-first century. Debbie, Jerry, and others at the Pow Wow were
kind enough to answer my questions though some of the topics were understand-
ably sensitive—when it came to medical ceremonies, burials, and the roll of intermarriage on clan structure. Any errors in the interpretation are mine alone. Again I
deeply thank all members of the Creek community in the Panhandle region.

I extensively used texts by David Lewis, Jr. and Ann T. Jordan Creek Indian Medicine Ways, and A Sacred Path The Way of the Muscogee Creeks by Jean and Joy-
otpaul Chaudhuri. I also used the Dictionary Muskokee and English by Rev. R.M.
Loughridge, D.D., A Dictionary of Creek/Muskogee by Jack B. Martin and Margaret
McKane Mauldin, and finally Creek Country The Creek Indians and Their World
by Robbie Ethridge.

My editor, Susan Mary Malone's, help as always was invaluable. A little harder
this time, Susan. Critical Readers Michael O'Reilly, Roger Spencer, my wife Gwenn,
Robert J. Fenwick, Kalyn Saunders, and mother-in-law Helen all contributed sub-
stantially to the quality of the final manuscript. To Kerry McQuisten and the staff at
Black Lyon Publishing: I am honored to be counted amongst one of their authors.

Finally I would like to thank the judges of the Romance Writers of America Cath-
erine contest and Senior Wild Rose Press Editor Stacy D. Holmes for valued direction in the rewriting process that is always a painful labor of love.

Chapter 1

Apalachicola National Forest

Crystal stumbled back from the river bank, grabbing for her grandfather's arm. Cold fear spiraled up her spine.

The dead man lay on his back in the shallows, a rag stuffed in his mouth. He was older, probably mid-sixties. A gaping wound across the pale gray of his neck, eyes wide open as if studying the cloud-spattered Florida sky, plaid shirt and jeans—torn, dirty, and stained. His blood-drained face was drawn and contorted, pleading for release from an unknown torment.

The last body she'd seen was her grandmother's lying peacefully in an oak casket. There was no peace today.

"Don't look into the eyes," her grandfather warned.

Crystal swiped a shaking hand across her mouth and fought the sour urge to vomit.

"Best not to rouse the *puyvfekcv* of the dead," her grandfather said.

Crystal swallowed hard as she studied the weed-infested river's edge for signs of danger, listening—sensing. Certainly in other parts of the world people were brutalized, but not here. Not in her life.

Hunch-shouldered, her grandfather turned slowly. Faded denim shirt and blue jeans-covered legs bowed from years of hard work. Most of the day had been spent gathering the medicinal herbs and roots needed to replenish his healing supplies. Fresh potions were best.

"There are tire tracks here in the mud." Crystal knelt next to the shallow river bank. "And some different ones back up there." She pointed to a clearing in the tangle of trees and undergrowth. Keeping her attention off the dead man helped push the bile back into her stomach, kept the immediacy of death at bay.

Her grandfather turned his wrinkled face. A light breeze moved long strands of grey hair across his cheek.

"The one up there turned around," Crystal said. "And, they're all new. Whoever did this isn't far away." The pounding in her head eased but a power, cold and unseen, gripped her throat.

Of course, her grandfather knew all that. He had taught her the craft of tracking, knowing the fresh trails and the useless ones. He was looking to the sky now, or maybe to the high hammock of dense pines and red oaks that made up the Apalachicola Forest. Unlikely they would give him an answer.

"His spirit will be restless. This is really bad, Grandpa," she said. Drops of sweat slithered down her back. She shivered.

He nodded and licked his dry lips. "Even white men search for peace, maybe not with nature and Mother Earth, but with something."

There was danger here, and no time for discourse. "This is a crime scene, a murder. We can't disturb anything. And we need to get hold of Sheriff Tumley as soon as possible … and we need to get out of here." Crystal retraced her steps from the wooded trail by which they had approached the river, her heart pounding. Until now this had been a happy place where generations had celebrated the wonders of life—births, weddings, harvests, and good health. Now dark, violent death swirled in the eddies of tea-colored water that flowed about the body and river reeds.

"Sheriff better get here soon," her grandfather said. "Gators'll get him before long."

"My cell phone should work as soon as we get back to the truck. If not there, then once we get to the highway. It'll be dark soon. We need to leave!" Who would do this? What could have led to such a death?

Blinking back tears, she peered into the forest. Up the ridge line, nearly silhouetted by the trees, a movement caught her eyes. Reflective tan metal, a vehicle, climbed away from the river. She took a slow deep breath. It didn't ease the squeezing in her chest. "Did you see that, Grandpa?"

"A truck, probably. Maybe an SUV." He squinted toward where

the vehicle must have come from and then glanced back to the west.

They were vulnerable. They had no weapons and her grandfather could not run—best to head away from the forest road ... hopefully away from any threat.

He knelt, brushed dirt aside, and picked up a piece of willow bark—hesitated—then discarded the piece as if it were contaminated. Rising shakily he held tightly his satchel of herbs, roots, sassafras, and wormseed they'd collected earlier.

"There must be a car down there too," Crystal said, fleetingly pointing to uniformly spaced marks in the ground. "The tire tracks go right into the river."

Her grandfather nodded and looked out over the water, his weathered face hardened.

"What?" Crystal asked.

"Might have been more," he said.

"What do you mean?"

"I've seen floating debris in the river a few times recently." He pointed a gnarled and bony finger across the meandering water to the opposite bank. "Out in the current. I didn't know what it was. No question today."

"You've seen other bodies?" Smoldering-hot anger and fear climbed into her throat, closing off her airway. "You should have told someone," she choked.

"Didn't think they were bodies until now." He held his grand-daughter's stare, then focused into the woods behind her. "We need to leave ... they're watching."

Crystal followed her grandfather's gaze. The sweaty hair at the nape of her neck springing up and down like the hairs on a frightened cat. "Who's watching?" She whispered.

Her grandfather picked up a canteen and his leather sack.

Her voice quivered as she repeated, "Who's watching, Grandpa, men or the spirits?"

"Maybe both." He was already halfway up the steep berm that separated the hiking trail from the river bed, his walking stick biting deeply into the moist soil.

Crystal glanced over her shoulder, the skin on her back tingling. Crunching gravel under her grandfather's boots brought visions of fleeing Creek ancestors, corn fields ablaze. Bronzed women, with swaddled babies weaving through the forest, terror etched in their faces.

Then she also scrambled up the crumbling slope and into the forest.

Chapter 2

North Fork Trail, Apalachicola National Forest

Grant Sands had never minded the baking sun during the war and he didn't mind it today. Somehow the radiant warmth always helped ground him, anchor his mind in the present, pushing the images of dead children and burning bodies back into the dark of night, back into his dreams and nightmares.

Today he was artifact hunting, reconnecting with the happiness of his youth, pushing away the stark reality of war. The freshly plowed fields and recent thundershowers gradually revealed eons-old arrowheads, turning them to the surface after centuries lost. The day had been productive—an excellent Hernando, several partial points, and pottery pieces that were probably Woodland-era Walton.

He rubbed his fingers along the sharp edge of the point in his pocket, saw through childhood eyes the furrowed face and prominent nose of his grandmother. Her calloused fingers guiding his small hands as she'd taught him the intricate art of knapping arrowheads —her gaze shifting out over the lush and fertile fields of his grandparents' Carolina farm.

Clumps of mud dropped off his boots as he picked his way along the North Fork trail toward his parked Jeep. Mid-afternoon shadows had already reduced the visibility for artifact hunting. The pine-straw-covered trail wove amongst loblolly pines through the national forest. Grant monitored underbrush as he walked, watching for rattlesnakes and water moccasins. Moccasins were the worst, and most aggressive. His military-style .45 rested on his hip, the first round loaded vermin shot. The rest were hollow-point personal-protection rounds.

Flashes of sunlight through the waving pines jerked his mind to blinding bursts of cover fire from Special Forces F-22 raptor rifles. Shaking his head, he continued up the trail.

Near the river, Grant was surprised when a knotted walking stick emerged from the brush-covered slope. His hand went to the holstered .45. An old man struggled onto the trail, gripping the stick for balance and pulling a worn, purse-string bag behind him. His hair was long, salt and pepper, tied to the sides like many of the local Indians.

Grant eased his hand from the holster and was about to wave when a young woman climbed out of the underbrush. She stood taller than the crooked old man. Her hair, also dark, was pulled back in a conventional pony tail, projecting from a khaki hiking cap. Prominent cheek bones and a sculptured nose under satiny skin captured his attention, striking actually. His damp shirt clung to his shoulders as anxiety mixed with the smell of his own sweat. She turned to Grant. Her gaze swept over him and then scanned the forest to both sides and the trail behind him. Something was familiar about her.

The old man smiled, raised his stick. "*Estonko.*"

"Hello," Grant returned the Indian's greeting.

The woman did not smile. She glanced behind her from where they'd come, neck muscles twitching. Her gaze dropped to Grant's gun, to his pack, and down to his mud-covered boots, a tight set to her lips. Her companion had given him a quick pass. She did not.

Wind rustled the pine trees high above as cool air rushed in from the Gulf of Mexico, typical of a Panhandle summer afternoon.

Grant smiled.

She wiped strands of hair from her sweating forehead and took the bag from the old man. She continued to examine Grant intently, focusing on his pistol. The twitch had now moved to the corner of her mouth. "Are you headed west, back to the trail head?"

"Yes," Grant answered as he approached, keeping his hands in view, not making any sudden moves. Old habits die hard. A tendril of hair hung down across her amber eyes. No makeup. "Can I help you with anything?"

The woman leaned toward her elderly companion. Her facial

muscles softened into smooth classic lines. A flowery fragrance tickled Grant's senses, though she was too far away for it to be her scent. She said something in a whisper that Grant didn't catch.

The old man stepped forward and offered his hand. "Sorry for the coldness of my granddaughter."

"No offense taken," Grant said. "You have to be careful in the forest."

Her chin rose ever so slightly, revealing burnished copper skin. She was most certainly a relative of the old man.

"I'm Grant Sands from Panama City."

The Indian elder shook hands with weathered boney fingers. "Will Blackrock." No attempt was made to introduce the woman.

"Are you alone?" she asked. Dainty, silver-feather earrings swayed lazily.

Odd question from a stranger. "And why do you ask Miss—?"

"Blackrock." She continued to study him. "Crystal Blackrock, Doctor Sands. We've met … at last fall's fund raiser."

"Yes, of course," Grant said as he shifted, feeling the coolness of a breeze drying the sweat from his neck.

"We found a body by the river," the old Indian said.

"A human body?" Grant asked as visions of rocky crags and dusty bloated corpses flared before him. The pit of his stomach twisted cruelly.

"Murder victim, most likely," the woman said as she again scanned the forest from which they'd just emerged. "We're not sure how recently, but not long ago. Have you seen anyone?"

"I'm just out of the fields up by the Jacobsen farm, artifact hunting." Grant pointed back up the trail to the north. "Haven't seen anyone … haven't heard anything either, except some thunder earlier to the west, not down this way." He glanced into the forest where the woman was continually looking. Was there a threat waiting in the tangled undergrowth?

"We need to contact the authorities, the Sheriff's Office probably," she said stepping closer. "It's going to be dark soon. Do you have a cell phone that will reach out of here?"

"No … well, I have one, but I don't get a signal until the trail head or thereabout."

She turned easily to her grandfather, the tightness out of her stance. Soiled jeans hugged a trim athletic figure. Her top was large and loose, a denim man's shirt. "We're unarmed," she said. "And we don't know where the killers are. I think we need to keep moving. Try to keep ahead of them."

"Did you see them?" Grant asked.

"They saw us," the old man answered. He also scanned the tall pines angling down the ravine. Not so much searching with his eyes, but searching none-the-less.

"And their trail's very new," she said glancing between Grant and her grandfather.

He must have raised an eyebrow or something to pique the woman. She took a step back and stared up into Grant's eyes, shook her head just once, and inhaled noticeably. "The wire grass was still bent and I saw no over-trailing on the tire treads whatsoever." She rolled her eyes at the old man. He patted her arm.

"Look," Grant said. "We need to get out of here and call the Sheriff as soon as we have a signal." He focused on controlling his breathing, listening.

"That's where we were headed," the woman said. "I take it you know how to use that .45?"

Grant dropped the clip and removed the vermin shot, leaving only hollow points. "Two tours in Afghanistan, ma'am, though these weren't very useful over there." He slammed the clip in place, and chambered the first round. The recalled hiss of whizzing bullets tried to unsettle him.

Her lips tightened. She nodded, turned and headed down the trail.

Grant noted the swing of her lean frame as she pirouetted, digging Frye boots into the pine-straw. Firm muscles propelled her up a rise, damp still from the night's rain. Crystal Blackrock was spunky, like his kid sister, Aubrey.

Now he remembered her from the Relay for Life the previous April, and the year before he thought. Her group had repeated in winning one of the team awards, though he could not recollect which.

A twig snapped back down the ravine. Grant's head swung instinctively … insurgents? Of course not, but threats nonetheless and the potential for death.

The old Indian fell in step behind his granddaughter. Grant followed, a familiar pressure pushing at the base of his skull.

Chapter 3

Apalachicola National Forest

Grant Sands was not the killer. The tightness in her neck eased. She recognized him from the fund raisers and from hospital-discharge summaries at her clinic in St. Joe. Doctor Grant Sands was not only an Indian-artifact collector, he was also an intensive-care physician, and apparently a veteran. He moved his compact frame deliberately with calculated agility.

He stayed in the rear, carried his pistol casually at his side, not holstered. His entire form pounded out the wiry and explosive confidence of a warrior. Crystal recognized the .45 as a semi-automatic pistol, similar to one her grandfather owned. It did help to equalize their situation with the murderers, by how much she was unsure. Guns scared her. She'd shot with cousins and her grandfather but never felt comfortable, either with the guns or with people shooting around her.

Methodically she scanned the tree lines, confident the swamp would prevent an assailant from circling around in front of them. She had felt the presence of the killers in the forest before they'd come upon the doctor. That feeling still lingered from back up the trail.

Doctor Sands also watched, pausing every now and then to listen. After about a quarter mile of hiking, he stopped, head swinging quickly to the left.

"Did you hear something?" Her pulse quickened.

He put a finger briefly to his full lips, raised two fingers to steely eyes, and then pointed into the forest, behind them and to the right. Purple shadows and a light fog obscured the visibility into the dense stand of timber, pretty under different circumstances.

He crouched as did Crystal and her grandfather.

Watching the trail, he moved next to them. "One, maybe two, clearly not used to following in the woods," Grant whispered.

"We're between swamps," Crystal said. "We'd have to be another quarter-mile up to make a run through the forest, north maybe." Someone really was following them. The burning in her stomach told her so.

"Yeah, that would work," Grant said. "We'd come out just west of the Jacobsen farm."

"Did your cell phone work there?" her grandfather asked.

A series of shots rang out. All three dove for the bushes beside the trail. Her grandfather flew backward. The rifle cracks echoed off the trees, obscuring their point of origin. Grant fired back twice. The shooting stopped. Crystal kept her head low. The doctor's weight pinned her legs and butt. Neither of them breathed. Her pulse pounded in her throat. Her grandfather lay several feet away, holding a bleeding leg with both hands, grimacing. She couldn't reach him.

Grant raised his head slowly without moving from Crystal. "I don't see anyone," he whispered. Piercing gray-blue eyes bore into her. His face chiseled with resolve, calm confidence likely forged in the fires of combat.

Her hands shook as she again tried to reach for her grandfather.

Keeping low, beneath the underbrush, Grant eased off of her. Firm muscles brushed her buttocks. He leaned close to her face, stubble from his chin nearly touching her nose. Her pulse quickened. What was he doing?

"Can you cover us?" he asked, sliding the .45 to Crystal.

She crept back the slide of the semi-automatic, checking to make sure a round was chambered, then nodded.

Rolling on his side, Grant assisted her grandfather behind a grouping of saw palmettos, removed a knife from his belt, and sliced the bloody jeans up to the thigh. Her grandfather gritted his teeth but kept quiet as Grant turned his leg first right then left, pushing gently.

Crystal winced, the burning in her stomach returned. "Doctor Sands works at the medical center in town, Grandpa." She swallowed hard and refocused down the trail. No movement.

Grant stared in Crystal's direction and then swung his gaze back to her grandfather's leg. "The bullet went through, not bleeding too badly. I don't think it hit the bone."

"No, it didn't," her grandfather said.

Grant looked him in the eyes. Then he began cutting the jeans in strips and reached into his belly pouch.

"Grandpa is a healer, he knows about these things," Crystal said. "He's dressed many wounds." She fought the urge to spray the forest with shots. They probably needed to conserve their ammunition.

Her grandfather adjusted his leg with a groan through pursed lips, and cleared his throat. "Thank you, Granddaughter, now let the good doctor do his work."

Crystal scrunched her mouth but kept watching the trail. "I don't think they expected the gunfire from us. Nothing seems to be moving out there. At least not in close," she said under her breath.

"We still need to get moving," Grant said. He placed a pressure dressing over both the entrance and exit wounds, neither of which was bleeding heavily.

Crystal edged up behind a pine tree, and holding the gun in two hands, leaned against the trunk. Nothing stood out. No unnatural movement or activity in the forest or back up the trail. The shooters had either left or were also lying low. Either way this was bad. Clearly, the killers were following them.

"Can you walk?" Grant asked.

"Some, probably. I'll need help though. Did your cell phone work at the farm?" her grandfather grimaced.

"Yes," Grant said.

"Help me up the trail some and into the woods," he said. "And then the two of you can cut through the forest to the farm and call the Sheriff."

"We can't leave you," Grant said.

Crystal looked at her grandfather, eyebrows raised.

"This isn't Afghanistan, Doctor," her grandfather said. "This is my country. If I don't want to be found, no one is going to find me in these woods." He wrinkled his nose and mouth in a forced smile.

"He's right, he knows the forest like the back of his hand," Crystal said. "It shouldn't be that long." There was no way, hampered by her injured grandfather, that they could keep ahead of any pursuers. And, struggling through the deep underbrush would be nearly impossible.

Grant helped her grandfather but it still took them fifteen minutes to get a quarter-mile up the trail and into the woods a reasonable distance. Crystal carried her grandfather's satchel over her shoulder and continuously stopped to sweep the trail behind them, listening for pursuers. Sweat bathed her shirt as she nervously shifted the .45 from hand to hand. Her grandfather managed the pain with minimal complaints, and they finally settled him behind a stand of short-leaf pines.

Her grandfather gripped her arm. His penetrating glare spoke to her of Creek rites of passage, of courage and loyalty. Stone-faced, he looked at the doctor.

"It won't take more than an hour, Grandpa. Get that leg comfortable and we'll be back before you know it," Crystal said.

Will Blackrock nodded and then pointed his head into the forest. "Get goin."

Grant rechecked the bandages. "The bleeding has pretty much stopped." He turned away and caught Crystal's furrowed brow. "What?"

"It's a good dressing. Not much blood," she said, immediately wishing she'd kept quiet. He probably didn't care about her assessment. "Look, he's right, we need to get going. No telling how many of them there are." Crystal stepped into the brush. Her grandfather would be fine. He'd been the solid center of her entire life. He had to be okay.

Grant followed but turned around thirty paces after leaving the Indian healer to check one final time.

"Where did he go?"

She turned, surveyed the trees and underbrush, and shrugged. "He'll be here when we get back." She noted the grove of live oaks sloping to the south and recalled the stand of palmettos just after a clearing of Indian grass as they'd left the trail. "Let's go. The sun's gonna set soon." She handed her grandfather's walking stick to Grant, who held the pistol pointed to the ground. "Thanks for being here," she added.

As he took the stick their hands touched—strong, confident hands—the kind she'd expect a war veteran or doctor to have. It seemed his character matched the hands.

KINDRED SPIRITS: THE HEALERS **13**

He hesitated momentarily, and then nodded awkwardly. With simultaneous sighs they turned and walked north, the setting sun across their shoulders, the fresh scent of pine unexpectedly heartening. They'd heard no further shooting. Hopefully her grandfather was safely hidden. She sensed he was.

•

The burning in Will's leg spread upward, throbbing and aching into his groin. But that was how he always dealt with pain. Internalize it. Spread it throughout the body so that the entirety of his being could destroy it like fire consuming a log. Scraping away the pine needles and topsoil he rolled two marble-sized balls of moist dirt and molded them into the entrance and exit wounds. This is how his grandfather had stopped the bleeding during the Greenstick Wars.

He would recover from the gunshot but the violence inflicted on the dead man in the river and the soiling of sacred-ground would require more, a solemn healing rite.

Will slid farther underneath the overhanging palmetto, pulled branches with him, and positioned them in a natural arrangement as his grandfather had taught him. He closed his eyes, breathed deeply. Numbness descended over the pain and his heartbeat slowed. He mumbled an ancient healing chant, and faded into the underbrush.

Mockingbirds dove from loblolly pines and circled a moss-covered live oak in a dance of territorial conflict, actions that had occurred in this forest since time began. Despite the presence of dark-spirits life went on, as would Will Blackrock and his granddaughter.

Chapter 4

South of Jacobsen Farm

Crystal marveled at how quietly Grant crept through the forest's ground cover. A natural or just trained really well?

He leaned in close to her. "It shouldn't be more than a mile to the fields."

"As the crow flies, you mean. It'll take a while cutting across here," Crystal said, quietly picking her way around fallen pine trees and growths of palmetto.

She'd never been off the trail in this part of the forest, not even when hunting. Grant led, taking long strides but silently ducking around bushes and tree limbs, careful not to slap her in the face.

After about fifteen minutes he stopped and crouched low, as did Crystal. He listened for what seemed like an eternity. "You work at a medical clinic?" Grant asked over his shoulder.

"The Family Medical Clinic in St. Joe," she whispered.

He nodded. "Your team won one of the fundraising awards at the Relay."

"Do you remember from the awards ceremony or the fry bread booth?"

His head shook. "Hey! All those trips weren't just for me. I was feeding half the event's chairpeople most of the night. That stuff is addictive, you know."

"Humpf," Crystal tried to squelch the sound. They rose cautiously together as both studied the forest behind them.

"You're Creek, right?"

"You recognized Grandpa's greeting," she said. "He sticks to his traditions."

"That's about it for my Muscogee dialect," Grant said.

"Well, you certainly have a stomach for the food," she said, absentmindedly, fretting over her grandfather.

"Yeah, well some things just get better with time."

Grant stepped lightly over a fallen pine and held Crystal's hand firmly as she carefully avoided the fallen branches. He plodded up the incline toward the farm. Clean cut, dressed in a SPORTIE nylon field shirt and pressed fatigue pants, lots of pockets. He didn't even smell bad after a full day in the sun.

She pulled at the bandana around her neck, letting more air flow against her skin. They were making good time.

He paused for her to catch up. "I don't know if anyone is at the farm, but we can still meet the Sheriff there."

"Do we have to cross a field?" Crystal peered back into the darkening forest. "We'd be sitting ducks out there for anyone with a rifle."

"There's a shelterbelt to the west near the road. We can move up to the farm house along it."

Ten minutes or so later he stopped once again, swung through a hundred and eighty-degree arc, listening more than looking. Jaw set firm, arms muscular and well-defined. Apparently satisfied, he turned to the north where the terrain began to decline.

She was reassured by his vigilance and probably a bit by the wide expanse of his powerful back. She looked down the slope. "We'd better head a little west here." Catching his eye, she pointed up a rise to their left.

His gaze briefly dropped to her sweat-soaked chest then diverted up the hill and finally back the way he'd been heading.

"I haven't been in this part of the forest before," Crystal said. "But I know there is a big swamp along the northern edge. If we go down that way, we're going to get wet." The last thing they wanted was to be trapped between their pursuers and the swamp.

Grant nodded. "Right, we need to move west a bit anyway."

Crystal pushed sweaty hair from her face and scrambled up through the forest. The trip was taking too long. She worried about her grandfather's condition, not just the gunshot wound. Grant followed her as bright sunlight sporadically broke through, temporarily blinding them to the shadows.

Near the ridge, she stopped and used the elevated position to survey the woodlands. "I see a break in the trees, maybe a quarter mile."

Grant stared back down the rise. "I don't think anyone is following us. Hope your grandfather is okay."

Nausea gripped Crystal. Her legs turned to noodles.

Grant caught her arm and eased her to the ground.

"Whoa," she said, shaking her head. "Not smart! I haven't drunk anything for hours. I'm usually better at this."

"Your face is flushed." He put his hand on her forehead. "And you're dry as a bone." Sitting next to her, he pulled a plastic drinking bottle from his belt. "It's an electrolyte solution. I've had three already today."

"Crap," she mumbled, took the bottle and swallowed a generous gulp.

"Yeah, it creeps up on you," he said, removing her hat. "You won't need this anymore." He poured water from another bottle into his hand and rubbed it on her brow as she continued to drink.

"Baptism under fire," Crystal joked. But the cooling effect was welcome.

He smiled —straight, white teeth —a thin scar on the chin. "Do you need to rest?"

Probably, but she was not going to be the fading female. "Pour some of that water on my head, I'll be fine." She stood, a little wobbly, not bad. They were wasting time and her grandfather needed help.

Grant emptied the bottle over her. Wet hair clung to her neck and water coursed down the front of her shirt. He looked away quickly, but not that quickly. "That way?" He pointed to a clearing in the hammock of trees where light filtered through.

"I'm right behind you, Kemosabe," Crystal said.

Grant smirked. "You can wait with the Sheriff's deputies when they arrive. I can lead them back to your grandfather."

So there it was, the macho male. "Don't take me for a lightweight, Doc," Crystal said. "I'm just not used to dead bodies and being shot at. I guess you are."

Grant snorted under his breath.

The tree line gave way as they approached a furrowed field. The pine forest yielded to a smattering of hickory, beech, and a solo grand magnolia tree. A fox squirrel jumped deftly from branch to branch.

Crystal used her cell phone to call Sheriff Tumley … twenty minutes away. She pulled up the old shirt to replace the phone on her belt. Smooth skin flashed at her hip and again his gaze lingered. Their eyes met and he quickly looked back into the woods.

While waiting on the Sheriff, they cautiously crept through the underbrush toward the road. Intense masculinity pressed close in behind her with a familiarity that was unsettling, as if she'd been in the forest with him before. Crazy.

"I told him we'd be south of the farm by the shelterbelt. There's probably pretty good protection over there." She looked over to Grant, silhouetted by the final rays of the setting sun.

"You didn't see the killers at the river bank, did you?" he asked.

"I saw a tan or beige vehicle moving up the rise to the north-west."

"But no individuals, I mean … like someone you could identify?"

"No, but Grandpa sensed they were near. I think."

"He's a healer, your grandfather?"

"Actually a medicine man, a *heles-hayv*." Crystal squinted at Grant. "He does other things, of course, to make a living."

"And your father?"

Heat rose into her cheeks and she felt her nose flare. "Long gone."

"Deceased?" he asked.

"No, just gone." Her head shook. "My mom is deceased … but my father really was never in the picture."

"Oh, I didn't mean to pry. I thought he'd be a medicine man as well."

"Apparently he didn't have the disposition. Mom was a Black-rock."

Grant nodded a few times, pulled on his lower lip, turned, and kicked the ground. "I've taken care of several patients from the St. Joe clinic. Do you know Herbert Sizemore? He has the pharmacy in St. Joe, I think?"

Smart, changing the subject. "*Wewahitchka*, actually. We do see him. He's lost some weight. It's really helped his diabetes. And Oswego tea has settled the stomach pains."

Grant scowled. "Oswego tea?"

"It's made from wild bergamot, one of our sacred medicines. It aids in digestion."

"Really?"

"Really," she said.

He rubbed sweat from his brow. "We almost lost him with that infected gall bladder, touch and go for a week." He squinted toward the setting sun.

She'd been short with him, biting almost. She swallowed hard. She'd made an unfortunate habit of being defiant with skeptics. Her grandfather always recommended walking in the other person's shoes before making judgments.

"Do you do clinical work?" he asked.

"Mostly, I run the business side of the clinic—taxes, payroll, and all." She drank the electrolyte. "It's a job."

"No clinical interests? I mean with a family history of native medicine?"

Her throat tightened like it always did with this conversation. She did come from a family of healers. But how did that fit into modern day America? Hell, even most of the young Creek thought she was wasting her time with all the ancient mumbo jumbo. And it wasn't just the sacred ceremonies and healing potions. The Creek had physically lost many of her generation to the big cities, technology, and intermarriage. What type of Creek Nation would her grandchildren have?

Hollowness enveloped her as she looked back into the forest where the morning had begun so beautifully. Where the spirits of her ancestors watched over her.

The Sheriff, another car, and an ambulance turned down the lane, lights flashing but no sirens. As the cars pulled up, Crystal turned to Grant. "Thank you for your help, Doctor." She pirouetted toward the approaching vehicles. "I'll be walking back to pick up my grandpa. You can stay with the deputies if you'd like."

Chapter 5

North Florida Panhandle

What a stubborn woman, he thought, although he'd never been very good at sizing up the fairer sex. The Sheriff had dropped him at the trail head to retrieve his Jeep and with a little bit of luck Will Blackrock would be on his way to the hospital soon. Both he and Crystal had a lot of questions to answer. Speaking of questions, he needed to stop by the medical center and get a turnover on his group's critical-care patients for his night shift.

He'd check on Mr. Blackrock later. Surely they'd take him to surgery to clean the wound. How long would the authorities keep Crystal? She must be exhausted. Though he had to admit, she'd rallied pretty well after resting and getting some fluids. Tougher than he'd first thought. Cute even in her field clothes, probably a real looker when cleaned up. No wedding ring, in her mid-thirties, parents deceased or gone. She could have a history.

Will Blackrock, on the other hand, was clearly a cornerstone of the local Creek tribe, a patient teacher much like Grant's grandmother. But teachers needed receptive students, willing to accept the challenges of learning through life's experiences. Elders with deep wrinkles, callused fingers, eyes of compassion and understanding could still only point the way. The young must embrace the journey, sometimes poorly prepared and often with dangers lurking in the darkness. Grant had certainly paid the price and stared into the gloom. What abyss did Crystal Blackrock face?

He skirted the north end of the county on Highway 20 through miles of timberland, crossed the Bailey Bridge over St. Andrews Bay into the small town of Lynn Haven, veiled in a starless night.

A quick shower at his bay-front townhouse and he was back on the road, down Highway 77 to the medical center in Panama City proper.

Heather, the off-going intensive-care charge nurse, greeted him on the unit. "Hello, Doctor Sands. Doctor Byron and Ginger are in the conference room. I'll have the rest of the charts together soon."

Grant slid the glass door open and entered the cluttered room. Tim Byron and the night charge nurse were busy signing charts and conferring. "How was your day?" Grant asked.

"Not bad. Ginger is pretty much up to date. We've got three new admits," Tim Bryon said.

"It's good to be busy. Any problems?"

"A few, we'll go over them at the bedside if that's okay with you?"

"Fine ... hey, Ginger, can you text me when a William Blackrock hits the floor?" Grant asked. "I don't think he'll come to us though, probably straight to the surgical floor."

"I'll keep an eye out. Coming through the emergency room, right?"

"Or a transfer from the operating room. Gunshot," he said.

She pursed her lips and frowned.

"A leg wound," Grant said. "He should do fine, really."

Rounds held no surprises and near midnight Grant settled in the dictation area to catch up on backlogged records. If lucky, he might actually get a few hours sleep before it all started again in the early morning. He enjoyed the routine, enough time off to artifact hunt, travel, or exercise. He had no wife—came close before Afghanistan but the overseas deployment and critical-care fellowship were more than Jennifer Winthrop would tolerate. Things might be different now, but that bridge had been burned. As much his fault as hers.

"Your chest X-ray on Mr. Morris is up, Dr. Sands," Willow Tulles said.

"Thanks, Willow." He ran his fingers through his hair. "How's his oxygenation?"

The petite nurse consulted a clipboard. "Holding steady at ninety-five-percent saturation since being intubated. Breath sounds are clearing too. It's about time, he's had a tough couple of days."

Grant nodded and turned back to the records screen. "Hey,

Willow, you're part Native American aren't you?"

"Seminole … half anyway."

"Do you know many of the Creek?"

"Sure, but there's been a lot of intermarriage over the years. So even those that are full-blooded Indian may be split heritage from different tribes."

"You don't have any Creek blood?"

She set down the clipboard and tilted her head slightly. "Not as far as I know, my other half is Dutch—my dad."

Grant pulled at his lower lip and rolled his chair in front of the computer-generated image. Mr. Morris' pneumonia *was* clearing up.

"There are always some Creek from the Wind Clan at the Pow Wows. It's a maternal line, you know? If your mother was Wind Clan, you're also of the Wind Clan."

"Yeah, I knew that. Kinda like being Jewish."

"I guess." She didn't smile.

Probably not his best stab at humor. "Do you know any medicine men?"

"Creek or Seminole?"

"Creek," Grant said. "I imagine the traditions are pretty specific to each tribe."

"Most medicine people don't open up much to outsiders, especially about the ceremonies—the chants. It's just not done." She pushed her chair back from the computer keyboard she'd been working on. "There aren't many left. The majority of the tribes follow mainstream medicine these days." She studied him under a single raised eyebrow.

"Healers pass down family lines, right?"

"Mostly—children are often picked at a young age. It's not always a man, you know. Some of our most revered medicine people were women." She tapped a pink pen against her clipboard, soft brown eyes waiting patiently.

Grant turned back to the charts, stretching his neck to relieve the tightness at the base of his skull. He made a mental note to ask his grandmother about Cherokee medicine the next time they talked.

Chapter 6

Community Medical Center Surgery Waiting Room

All in all her grandfather had done remarkably well for an eighty-seven-year-old with a gunshot wound. In fact, he had already returned to the trail before they arrived.

Sheriff Tumley had smirked at her grandfather. "Startin' another war, Will?"

"Crap," her grandfather said, wincing with each step.

Tumley swatted mosquitoes from his neck and pointed up the trail. "Hear anything recently?"

"Nothing for over an hour. They're gone."

Tumley let dirt fall between his fingers. "Still wet, we'll be able to find some tracks."

The paramedics unfolded a nylon stretcher and snapped together telescoping aluminum rods.

Shaking his head, Tumley had given one final look toward the river and spat off the trail. "We'll need to help you guys carry him back to the trail head. The body and tracking will have to wait till morning."

Presently, Crystal found herself lying across a set of hospital waiting room chairs. She curled a leg under one of the arm rests as the contoured blue plastic cut into her back. The television was off and she was alone, the last patient's family having left nearly an hour earlier. A nurse from the operating room had informed her that Mr. Blackrock was expected out of surgery soon after midnight.

Crystal knew that gunshot wounds to the leg were not the mundane problem typically seen in the movies. Lots of bad things could happen. Infections, blood clots, nerve injury just to consider a few. It would be hard to keep Will Blackrock down. Certainly, he understood the importance of keeping the wound clean and even antibiotics. But she had never seen him sit in a chair longer than to watch an episode of "Dancing with the Stars." And, farms were a hotbed of dust, dirt and manure. Not a good combination.

She slept fitfully, a hospital blanket over her shoulders and another one for a pillow. She would not be convinced of her grandfather's condition until she could actually talk to him. Eventually she gave up and walked about the waiting room, reading all the notices tacked on the announcement boards.

This was probably the same hospital where Grant Sands worked, though she had no idea what his schedule might be. Surely Intensive Care specialists had to do some night work. She imagined him administering to patients, putting in intravenous lines and managing ventilators, as well as dealing with distraught families.

It took special compassion to handle those situations well, not unlike being a medicine man or healer. A lot came down to "bedside manner."

There was a touch of sadness to the man though. She'd sensed it when he'd talked about guns and killing. He'd shown a brief look of foreboding. She'd seen that look in Native American veterans, their minds far away in war-torn countries. It always left her with a hollow feeling of helplessness enveloping her core. These men deserved reclamation. She just didn't know how to get the process started.

Her involvement with men over the years had largely been with outcasts who didn't deserve the same concern as these honorable vets. Probably, she had inherited her mother's addiction to wayward souls, those with no well-defined future.

Her mother died in an accident when Crystal was still in junior high school, no alcohol that time. God knows if there was anything else. Her grandfather never cried in front of Crystal, only that one lonely tear back so many years. He'd held her tight that night and simply whispered to her hair, "Fathers should not outlive their children."

Grant Sands would make a good father some day. She imagined him softly holding an infant in blankets, watching the innocent face and glowing with love. Where did that thought come from?

Crystal sat up. Had she been dreaming?

The door at the end of the room was open. Sheriff Tumley and a deputy stood looking at her. "Sorry if we woke you, Miss Blackrock," he said.

"No, I wasn't sleeping. Just catching a little catnap until the surgery finishes." She placed the blankets beside her as the Sheriff and deputy sat.

"You goin' home afterwards?" the Sheriff asked.

"I'll grab a hotel for a day or two. I don't want to be too far away."

The Sheriff glanced at the smartly dressed deputy who retrieved a notebook and pen from his pocket. "Can I get your cell phone number? I'd like to get back to the shooting area first thing in the morning, look it over, recreate the events, and recover the body."

"You need me to go? Well, of course you do. Who's going to show you where the body is?" Crystal's stomach ached, the tightness in her neck increased.

"Yes, and probably the doctor." Tumley chewed on something in his cheek. "It was too dark to see much when we picked up your grandfather and we'll need all the help we can to find where the shooting happened."

"I don't know how to reach Doctor Sands. But he'll probably be here at the hospital in the morning," Crystal said.

"He's here tonight. I just talked with him on his cell phone. He offered to drive you, unless you're goin' back to St. Joe when we finish."

"I'm sure Grandpa will be in for a few days," Crystal said. "I'm not sure I can leave him in the morning, he ... neither of us has anyone else to help."

"We'll have to work something out," the Sheriff said. "I would have preferred to recover the body tonight. The longer we wait, the fewer clues we'll find at the crime scene."

Reluctantly Crystal nodded and shrugged. "I'll try my best, Sheriff. But I'm all he's got."

"We'll see you early then." The Sheriff tipped his hat and nodded to the deputy.

Crystal gave the well-groomed deputy her cell phone number and home address as well as that of the St. Joe clinic. A wedding ring gleamed on his left hand, his conversation clipped and professional. His wife was lucky and probably deserved a good marriage.

She sighed.

"Doctor Sands said he'd meet you in your grandfather's room first thing in the morning." The deputy smiled briefly and then left. Crystal looked at her wrinkled and sweaty clothes. Would they dry by the morning if she washed them in a hotel sink? They'd better. Walmart was twenty-four hours but she was too exhausted to think of anything but a bed and a few hours sleep—maybe in the morning.

Of course, she could drive herself back out to the forest in the truck; it did pretty good handling mud and ruts. But she sure as heck didn't want to get stuck on some panhandle back road. Better to take the doctor up on his invitation. *Crap!* The gas traveling back and forth would be nearly forty bucks. But, she didn't relish the questions he'd throw at her about her native ways. The same ones she'd asked herself since her initiation. The ones her grandfather harbored but didn't ask anymore.

•

"Doctor Sands." Ginger interrupted his concentrated study of a patient's inputs and outputs. "You said you wanted to know when Mr. Blackrock was admitted. He's still in surgery but expected out within the hour. He'll go to room 3118."

He thanked her.

"The OR nurse gave me a grilling before she'd release the information," the charge nurse said.

"Why was that? Didn't you tell them I was requesting it?"

"I eventually had to. They'd gotten an insistent call at the front desk earlier asking about a gunshot victim. The caller didn't have a patient's name and claimed they were with the Park Service." Ginger leaned close. "Of course they didn't give out any information. With the gunshot and all, everyone was a little antsy."

Grant turned back to the tabulated columns. Who besides the Sheriff and emergency staff knew about the shooting? *Damn it.*

Chapter 7

Community Medical Center Surgical Ward

Her grandfather snoozed peacefully, thanks to the pain medication.

The white hospital sheets and blankets were a stark contrast to the bronzed and weathered skin on the back of his hands. Metal intravenous poles with clear plastic fluid bags and tubing surrounded his bed. It conjured some twisted reincarnation of medicine poles arranged on sacred ground. She imagined her grandfather meditating rather than sleeping. She had seen him in that state many times before. This was different.

The rising sun warmed Crystal's face as she stood at the window. Light painted patterns of yellow and gold across the far wall of her grandfather's room. The morning haze almost gone; it would be a hot, humid Sunday. She readjusted the starched new collar on the Jacqueline Smith top she'd purchased at Walmart an hour earlier, unsure if the irritation on her neck was from the new fabric or sunburn. Her pants had cleaned up well enough in the motel sink.

The old shirt was a lost cause from the start.

Today would be hard. She'd never handled death very well. And the disharmony of the murder victims' spirits was an affliction that would spread to Crystal if she became involved. The dead needed their eternal rest and at the ripe age of thirty-two, she did not feel compelled to dwell on mortality.

"Pretty blouse," her grandfather said as he gingerly repositioned his injured leg.

"Slim pickings at six o'clock in the morning." She smiled. "How you feeling?"

"Stiff." He struggled to sit up, mumbling under his breath.

Crystal reached for the bedside controller. "Let me raise the head up some, Grandpa." She also rolled the pillow behind his neck.

"That anesthesia stuff is horrible." He padded the bandages on his leg. "My healing chants sound like hurt dogs howling. It's a blessing there're no bones to spit from the wounds … I think the bandages would keep 'em from coming out."

"The nurse said the wound was dirty." Crystal pursed her lips. "They washed it out with saline—"

"Seawater. Man-made, but still seawater." He pointed to the plastic bags above his bed. "The dirt did its work. I need to do the chants to prevent infection though."

"They have you on antibiotics … it's in those bags," Crystal said.

"It may help. But the chants are what give nature—the salt, water, cotton, and medicines their powers. It's a delicate balance, and it is working." He smiled.

She repositioned the bedside chair to allow the full rays of the sun to bathe her grandfather's leg.

"They're going back out this morning?" he asked.

"Yeah, they want the doctor and me out there. I don't relish going back down those trails." Tightness gripped her lungs as she sighed involuntarily.

He frowned and the edge of his mouth wrinkled. Finally, he nodded and looked out the window.

"They want to examine the area of the shooting and the river," she said. "Doesn't look like you're going anywhere soon."

"You don't have to go down to the river," he said. "You can point out the stump from up on the trail. They'll ask a lot of questions. Where we first saw the body? How it was laying?" He stared out the window. "I told them about the tan colored vehicle."

"I think it was fairly large. The way it moved through the trees," Crystal said.

He held her gaze.

"I don't remember any sound though. The river is pretty quiet but I still didn't hear it … just caught a glimpse." Try as she could to remember more, she couldn't.

He sat up more in the bed. His tongue moistened his lips. "It would probably be best to get Micah Kanache to do a singing way for you ... It can't be helped." He padded the bed for her to sit.

Both of them would need a ceremonial cleansing after their encounter. Carnage and violence made it ever more imperative. Micah Kanache had helped many war veterans regain their harmony and escape the grasp of the dark underworld. The dead did not easily let go of their attachments to the living and frequently spirits needed help finding their eternal abode.

Crystal climbed onto the sterile bed and lay her head on her grandfather's shoulder. His hand gently brushed her clean, straight hair. "Go ... get it over with," he said. "I'll be fine."

Minute particles danced about in the stream of sunlight from the window. "I can hardly remember when we buried Mom and Grandma." Her grandfather's embrace eased the hollowness in her chest, full breaths of resolve and renewed confidence edged into her.

"Death and birth, the end, the beginning," Her grandfather murmured into her hair. "The passage of time has always been so important to men ... but it probably means nothing to the Creator and our blessed ancestors."

Crystal turned and studied the creases about his eyes, the bushy salt and pepper eyebrows. "It's hard, Grandpa —"

"Of course it is." He smiled. "Could it ever be easy for people to understand what it took to create the world?" He brushed a strand of hair back behind her ear. "If we can get a hint we are lucky. And ever-so-much more enlightened than most men." His face reflected the radiance of the morning sun. "That's worth a lifetime of sacrifice."

She snuggled more against his firm arm, absorbing the wisdom and determination.

"Sorry if I'm interrupting." Grant Sands stood at the open door. Crystal sat bolt upright, as if she'd received an electrical shock.

Her grandfather sucked in a quick breath as the mattress bounced his leg.

"Oh! Grandpa." Crystal grabbed his hand and held tightly.

He winced briefly then turned to Grant and winked. "You two watch out today. It's not just the spirits that are riled up."

Grant stood casually leaning against the door jam, his blue eyes strong and penetrating. Crystal smoothed the new blouse with her hands, a flutter stirring her stomach.

"We'll be with the Sheriff this time, should be a quick trip in and out," Grant said. "They said they'd bring their four-wheelers." He walked to the bedside. "How're you holding up this morning?"

Her grandfather extended his arms out, smiled. "All the comforts of home."

Crystal eased back down on the side of the bed and gently kissed her elder's hair. "I shouldn't be long, Grandpa. You give that leg a chance to rest. Anything I can get you?"

"If you see some haloneske, fresh roots would be great."

She gripped his hand and tuned to Grant. He was looking at her lips. Instinctively they parted as her tongue moistened them. A slight shift and he held her stare. Her pulse bounded in her temples. His gaze lingered, as did a fresh, earthy scent.

"Devil's shoestring," Crystal said. "It's great for treating varicose veins ... and gunshot wounds."

Grant turned to her grandfather. "No more surgeries planned for right now?"

"No, I think we've got a handle on it." He opened the bed-stand drawer and handed his leather medicine satchel to Crystal.

Grant nodded.

What did the nod mean? Agreement or simple deference to what the doctor considered unchangeable ancestral beliefs? Probably the latter. She held the sack tightly as a flush climbed up her neck. They never understood and generally the mainstream medical people were the worst. Her grandfather had explained that simple truth to her years ago but she still found it exasperating. Lately she'd come to realize the annoyance was as much a disquieting self-doubt as a resentment of other's beliefs. Did she have what it takes to be a medicine woman—a wife—a mother?

"They're expecting us at the trail head by ten. We've probably got time to catch some breakfast on the fly. Have you eaten yet?" Grant asked.

"No." Crystal shook her head and refocused. So the good doctor was clean, well dressed, smelled good, and considerate to boot. But what did he really think of the Indian ways?

Her grandfather turned his head slightly away from Grant with a mischievous smirk.

Crystal glowered at her grandfather. Grabbing her backpack,

which also served as her purse, she pointed a stern finger. "Behave, Grandpa ..."

Grant led her on a quick efficient trip through hallways, accessed by a pass card, and down stairwells to a windowless steel door. They were soon in the doctor's parking lot next to his Jeep CJ7. She threw her bag in the back and struggled, trying to get her hip up into the passenger's seat. Muscular hands slipped under her arms, fingers grazed the side of her breast as he effortlessly lifted her into the seat. A shuddering breath escaped her lips as the door closed.

Grant opened the tailgate and searched through his backpack. The sleeve of his shirt rose revealing a bleached-out tattoo—skull and crossbones. Odd. Not that he would have a tattoo, but a faded one that symbolized death. Was it another sign of a tortured soul?

He swung himself easily into the driver's seat, a man at home, in command. "All set?"

She adjusted the seatbelt. The shoulder strap slid snugly into the cleft between her breasts. His attention settled on her blouse. She arched a brow at him and his head snapped to the left as if he'd been slapped. He readjusted the rearview mirror and slowly backed from the parking place. Careful to avoid the white 300 class 4matic Mercedes sedan parked next to the Jeep.

Once on the outskirts of the city, he shifted expertly through the gears as they accelerated east toward the national forest. He glanced toward her chest, twice actually. The third time she caught his gaze. Sheepishly he returned his attention to the road.

"Not much scenery out this way," she said, breaking a smile despite her attempt to keep a poker-face. "With all the miles and miles of timber, I mean."

"Right, it's good to have some company, though the circumstances could be better."

"My grandpa and you seem to be taking this a lot better than me. I couldn't get the dead man in the river out of my head last night."

"Your grandfather seems to be pretty resilient."

"I don't know what I'd do without him. Or for that matter, what our tribe would do."

"Are there other medicine men besides Mr. Blackrock?"

"Just one ... up in Georgia, and he thankfully has an initiate."

Grant wrinkled his forehead. "What's an initiate?"

"A young person who is clean of spirit, and is selected by an elder to learn the medicine ways. It's a big commitment. And you really have to be up for the task."

Lazy swirling clouds crept inland from the Gulf of Mexico. Her mood lightened. She unconsciously picked at the small leather pouch around her neck.

"A nurse I work with—Willow, who's part Seminole—told me some of the best healers were women," Grant said.

"My great grandmother was a medicine woman, in the Oklahoma Indian Territory ... about the time my people were stripped of their lands. She held true to the harmony of nature, even in those worst of times. Many did not. Once a medicine person violates that trust, their medicine becomes bad and loses all power."

"There are bad medicine people?"

"Not so much today. But during the Trail of Tears, there were some. There was a lot of bitterness."

Grant shifted in his seat, moved his hands on the steering wheel to the ten and two o'clock positions, and glanced briefly at Crystal. "Will you be taking over for your grandfather, or will someone else in the tribe?"

Crystal sat quietly. Trees and underbrush flashed by as they drove northeast toward the forest. She breathed in the sweet, musky scent of live oak and Spanish moss. Felt the magic dampness as it nurtured the dense undergrowth.

She closed her eyes and allowed her spirit to expand into the natural world she'd grown to know so well. Tenderly she stroked the leaves and flowers—drifted effortlessly with a sparrow—plunged her hands into the fertile earth and inhaled the lavender fragrance.

Then she was back in the Jeep. "I don't know yet," she mumbled unheard toward the passenger's window.

Chapter 8

Surgical Ward

Adolescence had been tough on Crystal, a delicate stage the orphaned child had suffered through with little feminine direction. Will and his wife, before her death, had done all they could. Tirelessly they'd searched for tribal women to mentor her in the disciplines necessary to become a perfect woman. Sadly, the quality of direction and traditional gifts had suffered from that lack of feminine influence. And the mystical ability he and Crystal's grandmother had seen in the little girl was cloaked in a spirit sorely tested by the twenty-first century.

The ancestral conflict between red-stick and white-stick traits was ever present in Creek youth—warrior versus reflective, thunder and lightning versus harmony. Whereas women were typically favored with the white-stick psyche of introspection and reflection that had not been the path Crystal's mother had followed. Will constantly worried which traits Crystal would eventually exhibit. At least she hadn't ended up pregnant and drug addicted like her mother, but she did have her moments.

Ashley, his pixie morning nurse, peeked her curly head around the edge of the door. "Where's your granddaughter off to with Doctor Sands?"

"Police business I guess," Will said.

"Oh. Does it have to do with the guys that shot you? I suppose they'll be safe with the Sheriff and his men."

"I hope you're right." Will pulled himself up higher in the bed. The arthritis in his spine screamed with the muscle strain of repositioning the leg, too many years in the fields and forests. "When do I get the bandages off?" he asked through clenched teeth.

"We'll redress it before you leave … but Doctor McAlister is a stickler. He'll want to keep it covered until then." She shoved a stethoscope in her flowered scrubs pocket, set his chart next to the sink, and rushed into readjust his pillows. Finally she pulled the bedside tray closer, rearranging the water pitcher and plastic cup close to the railing.

Will thanked her as he eyed the railing.

"It has to stay up. Sorry, Mr. Blackrock. Those are the rules."

"It wouldn't be the first time I had to hop around on one leg."

She scrunched her nose and bit her lower lip. "Well, for today at least you need to call for assistance … we can't have any falls."

Will wished Crystal was still with him. She'd give him the leeway an elder deserved, maybe even help loosen the oppressive dressings. Here he was just another number, a statistic. His look must have offended the young nurse, who brushed her blond hair behind her ear as she studied him, deciding if he'd be cooperative or not.

"Doctor Sands is the chairman of our patient safety committee." She blushed. "I wouldn't want to be called in to explain a preventable injury to him."

Will was not convinced little Miss Ashley would have a problem being called to see Grant Sands. She'd likely prefer doing it over drinks though. "He's a pretty tough boss, I bet."

"No, no not really." She glanced out the window.

Will sensed sorrow.

She turned quickly back with a forced smile. "He keeps his professional and personal life pretty well separate."

She sighed, rubbed a hand across her chin, index finger along the corner of her mouth. "I don't think he has a personal life." She picked up the chart and stepped to the window, looking down into the parking lot. "I'm gonna miss the flowers this winter." She wrapped her arms around the chart. "That Doctor Sands, he has his Jeep and probably hiking boots … but that's about it. I don't even think he has a dog." She turned and left.

Great, his modern-day-challenged granddaughter was on an outing to a murder site with a socially conflicted war veteran. Maybe his grandfather's adage would apply "any experience that doesn't kill you makes you stronger."

He silently thanked the spirits that no bone splinters festered in his wound.

Visions of the sacred forest in better times enveloped him. His grandfather sitting with the shield of a long-dead Creek warrior directing sage and cedar smoke delicately into the night sky toward their ancient ancestors, imploring them to reveal the path to harmony with nature.

Quickly then in sequence he saw Crystal in agonizing self doubt, Doctor Sands anguishing over hemorrhaging and traumatized soldiers, and a dark-skinned robed man heartsick from human suffering. The first two he understood. The last was disturbing.

Chapter 9

Apalachicola National Forest

The Sheriff led the way down the North Fork trail with Crystal on the back of his four-wheeler. Grant and a burly deputy followed with a cache of weapons suitable for a small war. Crime scene technicians brought up the rear dressed in brightly colored vests embroidered with official looking letters and insignia. The backs of their all-terrain vehicles loaded heavily with tackle boxes of forensic equipment.

Three miles in the entourage stopped to study the trail maps. Grant stretched his legs while studying the surrounding foliage. Pine-straw crackled under the pressure of his boots as he crossed the trail. Bachman's sparrows watched curiously from the enormous branches of an ancient live oak.

"The spot where we picked up Mr. Blackrock is a few bends up," Sheriff Tumley said, comparing his GPS device to a folded park map. "And you said the shooting took place another quarter-mile in?"

Crystal looked up the trail. "Right, there should still be marks in the brush where we dove in. But it's several turns up the trail."

"Honestly, I think I'd have a hard time finding the place." Grant looked from Crystal to the Sheriff.

"We'll find it." Crystal wiped her neck with a bandana.

The deputies and crime technicians nodded, accepting Crystal's pronouncement with only tacit acknowledgement.

Grant stepped near the Sheriff. "Did anything come of the emergency room phone call last night?"

"The number ended up being a prepaid Walmart phone," Tumley answered.

Crystal frowned. "What about phone calls ... at the hospital?"

Tumley tilted his balding head slightly, his thin lips tightened. "The doc said someone, claiming to be from the Park Service, called the ER last night trying to get information on a gunshot victim." He glanced at Grant, bushy eyebrows raised. "They didn't get any information but the ER gave Dr. Sands the third degree when his nurse called later for information."

"It was the killers ... " Crystal said.

"We just don't know, Miss Blackrock. But we'll keep digging." The Sheriff swung a long leg over the four-wheeler, and addressed one of his deputies. "Kevin, why don't you take the lead with Miss Blackrock? If that's okay with you, ma'am?"

Grant handed a bottle of electrolyte solution to Crystal. "Sorry I didn't tell you about the call earlier." He detected a shiver as Crystal took the bottle, avoiding eye contact. Instinctively he reached a hand to comfort her. She'd turned to the deputy's four-wheeler and Grant simply continued the gesture to assist her onto the back of the Honda.

•

Crystal gripped mercilessly the hand-holds on the back of the ATV. This was going from bad to worse. The machine jumped unpredictably as the deputy negotiated roots and pine-straw-covered holes in the trail. Bad enough the murderers had seen them at the river and shot at them, now they were being hunted down by the same thugs. Her throat tightened.

"That didn't sound very good!" she yelled to the deputy over the rumble of the engine. "Does my grandpa need protection?"

"We had officers in the hospital and at your hotel last night." He smiled back over his shoulder. "Followed you to Walmart this morning."

"Really, I'm glad I keep my shades pulled."

The deputy nodded.

So, the murderers were worried about what she and her grandfather knew. Why hadn't Grant said something sooner? Was he lamely trying to be protective? She had sensed the concern when he brushed her hip at the rest stop. He had intended to do more, to rub her shoulder and tell her everything would be all right. It was her gift. She understood people, their fears, pain, and suffering.

She also recognized caring and compassion, even if it was misdirected and unnecessary. She'd felt his compassion the day before, but had discounted it as heightened sensitivity stemming from the violence.

Her grandmother had recognized early on that Crystal had the gift to know, a person the Creek called an *owalv*. She also told Crystal she might one day develop the psychic powers to be a main medicine woman. But still, in her thirties, Crystal labored with the commitment and responsibility. One had to believe. Not only in the mystic healing bond of man and nature, but also in one's own ability to control the gift for good. It was a life few could comprehend, let alone master.

"There, that's where we left the trail. Just this side of the stand of palmettos." Crystal pointed to a grouping of pines with an undergrowth of lush palms.

The mechanical rumbling quieted and the Sheriff signaled all to stay back as he and Crystal approached the site. She showed Tumley an area where the pine-straw carpet had been pushed up. Looking to the northwest, she quickly found evidence of blood on twigs and pine needles. As she turned, the Sheriff presented her with a shining, spent .45 cartridge.

"Good work, ma'am." He waved Grant over. "Which direction did you fire and how many rounds?"

Grant turned 180 degrees. "The sun is all different and the forest doesn't look the same ... I'm pretty sure it was to the southeast there." Grant pointed at an acute angle down the trail.

"I think so," Crystal added. "Maybe a little more to the right, but I was in a bad position to observe, actually." She smiled at Grant.

The corner of his full mouth raised, sparks dancing in his blue eyes. "I fired two shots."

"Should be another casing 'round here then," the Sheriff said. "Kevin, take one of the techs up the trail there to the right and see if you can find where the shooter may have been. Cordon it off and leave someone posted there." He then arranged for the rest of the group to continue up the trail.

The pit of her stomach liquefied as they approached the murder scene. Her saliva thickened and became bitter. They descended the berm on foot. Grant held her hand reassuringly as she half climbed and half slid down to the river level. The welcomed assistance eased her anxiety and a drink of electrolytes cleared the foul taste from her mouth.

The joy and hope that normally resonated at this sacred site now yielded to the unrest and disharmony of the dead. Crystal stopped at the bottom of the berm and did not approach the river's edge. The sick feeling in her abdomen engulfed her. "The body was in the shallows over by that cypress." She pointed to a large, dead tree stump next to the river. "The tire tracks are back up near the tree line. They may have come in on the old forest road."

Her breaths came in spasms as she fought to gain control.

"Kevin," the Sheriff said. "We'll need to cordon off a crime scene up on the ridge line road as well."

"That's where we saw the tan or beige vehicle my grandpa mentioned." Crystal hugged her arms to her body stiffly.

"And you heard nothing as you approached from the northeast, Doctor?" the Sheriff asked.

"Thunder, but no engine noises, no gunshots."

"How long were you and your grandfather at the site here, Miss Blackrock?" The Sheriff held a notebook and jotted numbers from one of the officer's tape measure.

"I told you last night, not more than five minutes." Crystal tried to keep the fear and frustration out of her voice. She jabbed a finger toward a shadowed tree line. "We came out of the forest over there. Walked the river bank to where we found the body." Cramps gnawed at her stomach. "When we saw the tire tracks we knew we had to get out of the area."

Grant put his arm firmly around her. The vibration in her arms stopped. Had they been shaking? She let her head settle gently on his shoulder as the Sheriff and his crew began the painstaking task of securing and evaluating the crime scene. The shoulder felt firm and reassuring. Her breathing slowed.

Tumley turned to Crystal after conferring with a senior deputy. "There's no body."

"What?" Crystal tore loose from Grant's arm and strode toward the river bank. "It was right there." She pointed into a pattern of water grass. "About three feet out, face up." *What now?*

"The current's not that strong here," the Sheriff said. "A gator must have gotten it during the night … if that's the case it won't be far. The water's clear. I'll have divers come in by the forest road. They'll find it."

"It was here." Her face flushed.

"Oh, I don't doubt you, Miss, this won't be the first," the Sheriff said. He wiped his mouth with a tobacco-stained handkerchief.

Crystal stared at him.

He looked away.

"There've been more murders?"

"Mostly missing persons."

"Mostly, what's that suppose to mean?" Crystal's heart rate slowed but the gnawing pain in her stomach continued.

"Sorry. I'm not at liberty to comment further, ma'am." He walked back to where a crime scene technician was studying footprints in the mud. The man stood no taller than Crystal, short-cut military-style hair. He pointed back into the forest as the Sheriff nodded.

So what her grandfather had said about bodies in the river was true. No point bringing that up to the authorities, if they already knew. Her heart ached as her mind turned to her grandfather. His sacred ground was surely not far from this desecrated place. The evil that had intruded into the sanctity of this forest would have to be banished and cleansed. And that would not be a simple task.

"Vehicle was probably a truck, from the tire tracks." The Sheriff wiped the handkerchief across his neck. "Could be a large SUV … not a common color for SUVs though."

Chapter 10

Florida Panhandle

Grant glanced furtively at Crystal staring out the window of the Jeep. Shadows stretched across the plowed dirt road leading them out of the forest. He searched the tree-line for deer. With dusk approaching they'd be stirring soon. She sighed but continued to gaze blindly, hurting.

"That was tough. I'm almost glad the body wasn't there, for your sake," he said.

At first he wasn't sure if she'd heard him.

Then she looked up through red and swollen eyes. "It's awful; they have destroyed a wonderful healing ground that may never be recaptured." A tear stole down her cheek and she turned quickly back to the window.

What drove the life of this beautiful but troubled daughter of the Creek Nation? A deeply shrouded and meaningful yet tortured soul. He pulled himself back from his thoughts. "What exactly is sacred to your people, the whole area or just the river?"

"The whole area really. Much of the washing and purifying of roots, bark, and leaves was done with river water right there at the edge of the glen." Her eyes shown amber—golden even—in the light of the setting sun. "This may have bad consequences for all of us." The deep furrows between her brows belied her young age.

He briefly checked the road ahead. "You seem pretty certain of that."

She swallowed and hesitated. "I sense danger and turmoil. And my senses are more often than not correct."

"Sounds pretty foreboding, anything more specific?"

"You mean, if I look in my crystal ball, can I see where it will happen?" She concentrated on her circling hands. "Or what the next six lottery numbers are?"

Heat rose up Grant's neck and centered behind his ears. "Sorry —didn't mean to ruffle your feathers."

"Yeah, I get that a lot. Generally, for people to believe, they want details." She looked at Grant, lips tight, and exhaled deeply through her nose. "Gut feelings don't get much respect."

This was not going well. Grant slowed as the forest road intersected a paved highway. Braking, he turned to Crystal. The specks in her eyes danced like tiny fires. He swallowed. "I'm sorry. I didn't mean to be insensitive."

She actually smiled. "You're not very good in an argument are you?"

"Were we having an argument?"

She shifted on the seat and resolutely held his gaze. "Creek medicine is a bond between man and Mother Nature. It has been passed down since time began and involves concepts of place, time, and wellness that defy modern scientific theory. That's okay with us. We accept these beliefs on faith in our ancestors."

"I give up." Grant spread his fingers and raised his hands off the steering wheel.

She blushed. "You're too easy."

Apparently the battle raging within Crystal Blackrock was fully capable of enshrouding both of them. With the teasing, a cute crinkle touched the edge of her nose. His heart thudded against his ribs. He swallowed hard, uncomfortable with sensations he'd not felt in years.

She examined him like an injured bird, the corner of her mouth twitched upwards.

Grant shifted in the bucket seat and pointed up the paved road to the northeast. "Right, I think is the fastest way back to town ... But we haven't eaten yet and it'll be dark in a few hours."

"Actually, I wasn't able to get the roots for my grandpa. I know he has some in his storage shed. It's just about ten miles southeast. We'd left some rice with venison fry sausage in the refrigerator. No point letting that go to waste."

"I'm invited for dinner?" Grant let his jaw drop.

"Don't get your hopes up, Doc. I'd look at it more as a bribe,"

Crystal shot back.

Grant laughed as he directed the Jeep southeast. The reflection of her smooth olive complexion overlaid the road in the front window as she dialed her cell phone to check on her grandfather. He quickly shifted through the gears and headed further into the outback of the panhandle.

Will Blackrock reported that no further anonymous inquires had been made at the hospital.

•

Crystal watched the familiar rows of young to mature pines flash by as the miles quickly passed. She used the long stretch of road to settle her mind.

"If you turn left on the dirt road just past the fence line," Crystal said. "My grandpa's house is about a mile and a half in."

"Is it a ranch or farm?"

"Mostly a farm, but he does run some cows and sheep." She shifted on the seat to face Grant. "The whole eastern and part of the northern edge of the property borders the national forest. Often we just ride the horses out into the forest."

Grant scanned, from left to right, the ridgeline she'd been pointing at. Then he repeated the process more slowly from right to left. "Does your grandfather have weapons?"

"Because of the calls, you mean?"

"If you're gonna be out here much, alone or with your grandfather, you should have some protection. A perimeter alarm would be good too," Grant mumbled as he continued to scan the farm, pasture and tree line.

"Like in Afghanistan?" Crystal said.

His face went pale, eyebrows dropping as did the edges of his full mouth. He stared down the dirt road. "Yeah, I guess."

"You don't like to talk about it. I know that from the war vets in the tribe. Most of them are from Korea and Vietnam though."

Grant continued to stare.

Her stomach turned and tumbled. Then a tightness rose into her chest—it was his feelings, his distress. Crystal was caught off guard. The aching was tremendous, overpowering. She had never experienced this physical bond with anyone other than close family. And even then it had never been this intense, this all encompassing. It wasn't right. He wasn't even Indian.

Chapter 11

Blackrock Farm

Shadows surrounded them as they approached the turn into the Blackrock farm. Grant's mood lightened as the gloom gave way to the light of open pasture. His stomach fluttered as he realized he would be here after dark with Crystal. She had invited him to her home.

He rolled down the window and inhaled the sweet fresh scent of hay, the smell of abundant feed and water. Plump cows raised lazy heads as the Jeep passed. His mind began to clear and his stomach settled.

"That's the west quarter." Crystal pointed past the cattle to a distant fence sloping down to wetlands. She twisted in her seat, stretched her neck and shoulders as her left hand absentmindedly rested on the gear-shift.

"How many head?" Grant asked, relieved to have the conversation off the war.

"Sixty or so, nearly as many sheep and a few goats."

She was studying him, looking for the cracks, the damage. And it was there, just beneath the surface. He'd never been very good at covering the evidence. But if you didn't let people close to you, they didn't notice. It had worked well the past few years.

"Here?" Grant asked as he turned the Jeep. They wound up an elevated road through a stand of cypress bathed in dark, pungent swamp water.

"Welcome to Blackrock. That's what all my kin call the farm, for as long as I can remember." Crystal waved a hand from east to west in a sweeping gesture.

"Your clan, is that right?" Grant asked.

"Yeah, you can call them our clan." Crystal paused. Grant waited. "Mostly we're from the Wind Clan, maybe some Bear also." She smiled widely.

"Is the property laid out by sections?"

"It was. Grandpa's farm is really a combination of several older homesteads. Some quarters or plots were sold off before he bought them, mostly the better farming land. We've got some acreage in crops but most of it's swamp or pasture."

"It's beautiful." Grant breathed deeply. Peacefulness dissolved the sharp edges of his awareness. "How far to the house?"

"The trees and swamp give way just past the old sawmill and then the homestead is up a rise near the creek. It's hard to see from the road."

"Must be around a thousand acres?"

"Nearly fifteen hundred actually, but only about nine hundred is really usable."

"Do you have family near?" he asked.

"Not really … a mile and a half or so."

He pulled at his lower lip. Tiny wrinkles edged from the corner of his eyes.

"Blackrock is part of the original Creek homestead property." She sighed involuntarily. "Grandpa has worked with several of the tribe to try and repurchase much of the original tribal lands that border the forest."

"Trying to keep the tribe together." Grant smiled.

"As best possible and for as long as possible … it is really difficult."

"It can't be cheap."

"I've worked with Nick Tulun at Florida First Realty to get financing as best we can," she said. "Who knows, maybe we'll build a casino."

"Oh! I truly hope not." Grant leered at her. "I work with Nick's father, Gabriel."

Crystal looked up toward the roof in thought. "A stroke doctor."

"Well yes, a neurologist actually. They're the ones that take care of the stroke patients."

"Great! Another thing to worry about," Crystal said. "That can happen after anesthesia, right?"

"It can, but if it does we typically know it immediately after the surgery. So ... I think your grandfather is out of the woods with that one."

She seemed to ease back in the seat as they approached the farmhouse.

•

Grant's gaze moved quickly, taking in the sights that comprised Blackrock. This was not a calculating combat analysis as Crystal had expected from the war veteran. No, the doctor's nostrils flared and his head rocked gently from side to side. He was not reconnoitering the property, he was feeling, smelling, and tasting the essence of Blackrock—a sensual connection that caused an uneasiness in Crystal. As if he were subtly invading her privacy.

"What do you think?" she asked as they crested the rise to the house.

Grant stopped and opened his door. He surveyed the house, workshop, and out buildings. Rough-hewn planks and wood shingles from the previous century. "It's a traditional Creek compound."

"Well, yeah ... what did you expect?"

"Hey, I didn't mean anything by that." Grant rubbed the back of his neck. "I wasn't expecting the building arrangements to still be like the 18th century." He shifted his head up the rise and shaded his eyes against the setting sun. "That must be the current farm house up there," he said nodding to a stuccoed ranch-style home.

"My grandpa and grandma built it shortly after my great-grandmother died back in the early 60s."

"Is she buried in the old log house down by the sheds?"

She nodded. "Yes ... she is, along with my great-grandfather who died a few years after the new house was built." Why did this obviously troubled vet focus on the ancient dead?

Grant walked a few paces to see the side of the old house.

"So, you know the Creek buried family members under houses—"

"And then frequently moved out to a different house," Grant added. "Is your grandmother buried down there too?"

"Fourteen years ago next month." Crystal closed her door and pointed toward the new house. "Are you hungry?"

Grant turned from squinting into the sun. His pupils rapidly dilated, drawing Crystal in. For a brief moment the breeze smelled of lilacs and the sun's rays teased her eyelashes. The scar on his chin spoke of lost friends and loved ones. Just as quickly their gazes diverted, the vision broken. These were emotions Crystal commonly absorbed from people, mostly relatives.

He turned and walked toward the covered pavilion, which by Creek tradition sat in the middle of the compound. "Let me look around a bit. I'll be up in a few minutes."

He reached into the Jeep and retrieved his .45. This would be more than an anthropological expedition. The war veteran was back.

While the venison heated on the stove, Crystal walked down to the old cookhouse cellar and retrieved a cut of roots from the Devil's Shoestring. Last year's would just have to do for her grandfather's potion.

He'd always been meticulous about his potions. She'd seen other medicine men use herb-filled sacks right to the bottom, sometimes with sprinklings of forest dirt mixed in. Will Blackrock had his own way. She wasn't sure it made a difference to the outcome, but it made a difference to her grandfather.

Climbing out of the weathered shack, she saw Grant standing and studying the wetlands to the west, the .45 tucked in a holster against his back. She approached quietly from behind, sure he would hear or sense her.

"There are no smells like this in Afghanistan," he said. "It grounds me, takes my mind and soul away from that God-forsaken place." He turned, his tanned face capturing the afternoon sun and radiating contentment. "Your perfume doesn't hurt either," he said. "The perimeter is clear. The only way in is up the road through the swamp or out the forest to the back of the house."

The change was so abrupt Crystal wasn't even sure she'd heard the revealing comments. Had she imagined that quick glimpse into the scars that were Doctor Grant Sands? "Was it really bad for you, over there?"

His broad shoulders noticeably tightened. And the glimmer in his eyes faded completely, but his facial expression never changed. He looked back to the wetlands and inhaled deeply.

When he once again turned to Crystal, a slight gleam inhabited his piercing eyes. He tilted his head in a half-shrug and simultaneously raised an eyebrow and allowed a pitiful smile to crease the side of his mouth.

"Is the food ready?" he asked.

"Yes," she answered softly as a breeze pushed hair against her cheek.

They walked together toward the house, her head at his shoulder level, a whiff of unadulterated masculinity curling about her. She looked down at his strong hand. How would it feel to hold? Would she feel secure and protected or would she be the resilient one, giving him the strength and support he needed? Could she even do that? Or was she destined to have her mother's bad luck with men?

Darkness crept in as they finished dinner. Crystal rinsed the dishes as Grant sipped a glass of merlot. The tightness in her neck had eased, probably the wine. There was lightness to her breathing. The clean crisp air had kicked the sourness out of her stomach. She felt Grant's gaze on her back, odd being in the farm house with an unfamiliar man. She needed to get back to the hospital, back to her grandfather's side. She wasn't sure why that urge gripped her. Was it concern about her grandfather or about her attraction to Grant?

Chapter 12

Blackrock Farm House

"I have to change my clothes and pack an overnight bag. I'll just be a few minutes."

"I'll be on the porch. Best to come out through the front screen door when you're ready," Grant said. In a hostile engagement you needed to know where the friendlies were, because all the rest were enemies. The mere thought of clandestine planning brought a heaviness to his heart. He was a physician, by God. It wasn't his role to kill the insurgents. It hadn't been his role in combat either. None of that had mattered when the AK-47s and rocket-propelled grenades rained down on him and his dead and dying squad members.

Water ran in a back bathroom as light filtered through an oilskin shade. Grant scanned the fence line and down to the Creek compound. Movement out of the corner of his eye refocused him around the corner of the house. Night blindness prevented him from seeing well into the forest and then again he caught the movement. A shadow behind the shade stood, arms raised, removing a blouse and bra. With slight turns, Crystal revealed her trim torso and breasts, whose firm erect outlines were not hidden by the shadowy veil. She sponged herself with water from the sink.

He'd rarely looked at women this way since his return from the war. Pursuits of pleasure had given way in his life to just trying to get through each day and keeping his wits about him. Loud noises and unexpected surprises still strained his control. That was getting better though. Or so he told himself.

The light turned off, scraping and creaking came from the interior of the house.

The screen door moaned lightly. Crystal stood in the shaft of light, inhaling the aromas of the farm. Grant longed for the contentment that showed on her face. A whiff of oatmeal soap mixed with wild flowers teased his nostrils. He'd experienced fragrances from nurses in the hospital these past years. But the subtle strength of Crystal's essence in contrast to the forest and farm left him unsettled.

"It smells like rain. I love the crisp freshness," Crystal said.

"I think you're right," Grant replied, though his mind was still on the powerful impact of her femininity.

•

He was troubled, that was for sure. But it was more than that. Crystal turned toward him, aware that the coolness of the night might reveal too much beneath her light top and bra.

"We have to assume the killers know all about your grandfather by now," Grant said. His gaze bounced from her bosom to her eyes. "You think they're still after him? Why wouldn't they be three states away by now?"

"They've got something here that they want to protect or hold on to." Grant fingered the gun on his hip. "That's the way it was in the war zones. If the insurgents hung around they were protecting something, maybe just an arms route. But something, or like you said they'd fire and be long gone before we overran their position."

Crystal shivered. "They might know about the farm too."

"How many Blackrocks in the area?"

"Just a few out here, several more in Apalachicola and Tallahassee. Most of us are online though ... have cell phones and all."

Grant studied her, probably considering the risks. But Crystal could also detect a softening of the hard shell. What was underneath? What had he been like as a young boy, as a young man before Afghanistan? War changed men forever. Charlie Silvers, a Vietnam veteran, used sleeping pills every night since the war, heavy ones. Though some were deeply scarred for life, many successfully re-assimilated to civilian society. Or was that just a shell, a façade they put up to get through each day?

"Best not to stay here too long," Grant said. "And when we get back to town I think we should change you to another hotel. Register under a different name."

"You think all that is necessary?" Crystal stepped closer, not sure why. His height was accentuated as she found herself looking up into a handsome, stony face—set with resolve. His breath, heavy on her cheeks, hinted of musky maleness.

"You can't be too careful ..."

In life and death situations he didn't have to add. After all, there were already probably two or three dead. A few more would probably just be the price of business to these guys.

She reached for his hand, held it with both of hers. The contrast was marked. Hers soft and petite, his man-sized, tanned, with strong dilated blood vessels. Hands made to work, to operate, to cure. Her abdomen fluttered as she thought what else they could do. "Thank you for driving me today ... And thank you for checking on my grandpa."

He looked down at their hands, exhaling through tight lips. Then he brought his other hand to engulf hers. A quiver ran up her arms. She felt like a child on Christmas morning—excited, expectant, and enchanted. These were protective hands, coarse to the touch in an erotic way.

"I'm sorry the two of you are involved in this." His grip on her increased. "I'm happy to help though, where it might actually make a difference."

Not like Afghanistan, she thought. The scarred warrior was back. Crystal could see the hurt in his eyes, but also a suggestion of something more: Powerful shoulders, taut muscles, and a tight set to his jaw. Scarred or not this was a man who still had fight in him, a man who still had the capacity for love and compassion, even if he didn't know it.

Grant had impeccable character—nothing like her father. She felt a flicker of hope in her core. Perhaps she could avoid the trap her mother had fallen into with men, if she had a man like Grant Sands.

He smiled down at her. The shell was cracking. What would she find beneath?

•

Grant wanted to take Crystal in his arms. Hold her securely and whisper that all would be well. Feelings he had not had in years. She had a mystical magnetism that drew him in. "It'll be all right. We just have to be careful."

She began to answer as his attention suddenly diverted toward the old log house. Lights from a vehicle reflected off the dilapidated roof line. "Are you expecting anyone?"

"I don't think so," Crystal answered. "My aunt knows Grandpa Will is in the hospital, but I don't know why she'd come out to the farm."

"Do you have guns and ammunition in the house?"

"A .270 Remington deer rifle and a twelve gauge," she said, as she surveyed the entry road. "I don't recognize that vehicle."

The crunch of gravel came closer. He'd been holding his breath. He squinted, straining to see. Luckily he'd been looking away from the house during their conversation. His eyes were accustomed to the dark. An SUV of some style. It would be in the compound next to his Jeep in less than a minute.

"Get the guns and meet me out back," he said. Bending low to prevent any silhouetting of his profile, Grant edged into the moist drainage ditch next to the house.

"Is it them?" Crystal asked as she silently slipped through the screen door.

"We're not staying to find out, douse the lights."

Muted sounds told Grant that Crystal was moving through the rooms. He crept to the back of the house and eased part of his head around the side of the dark eastern exposure. The house lights went out just as the vehicle stopped. Three shadowy figures emerged, weapons clearly in their hands. Definitely not Crystal's aunt. A muffled squeak told him Crystal would be on the back porch. He crawled to her and held a finger to his lips, then pointed to the woods.

The moist grass made no noise as they raced across the open yard to the forest, sheltered from the approaching assailants by the ranch house. A large man came around the far end of the house in a crouch. Crystal knelt behind an overgrowth of running oak just beyond the yard. Grant leaned down low and peered over her shoulder up toward the house, struggling to control his raspy breathing.

"I called 911 and left a quick message for Sheriff Tumley," Crystal whispered.

Grant gave her a thumbs up. Good—quick thinking. He glanced at the nearby trees and holly bushes, not much cover. They would have to move downhill into the forest to keep in the thick underbrush. Crystal grabbed his arm and pointed back toward the house. The man was looking directly at them, a glint of reflected light emanated from his face. Night vision goggles.

"Run!" he said, and pushed Crystal into the underbrush behind a grouping of pines.

Shouts in a foreign language came from the top of the hill. Bullets thudded into the trees on their right. Crystal sprinted through the woods. Grant barely kept up. She surely knew the area as she unhesitatingly angled downhill and to the northwest. A stinging in his hip caused him to stumble. The gunshots stopped.

He caught up to Crystal about a quarter mile into the forest when she stopped behind a large pine trunk to check on him. His right hip ached. A wet sticky feeling ran down his pant leg.

Chapter 13

Forest Behind Blackrock Farm

"Are they coming?" Crystal asked as Grant stood bent over breathing heavily. The rustle of leaves and snap of breaking twigs had halted immediately when Grant arrived. Little light from the night sky filtered into the heavy hammock of trees. She could just make out the drops of perspiration on his forehead, could smell his sweaty fear. They both remained still, ears tipped up the slope from where they'd come. Slowly the music of crickets and the hoot of an owl returned. No human noises except their own labored but restrained breaths.

"They will," Grant said. "As soon as they reorganize. We need to contact the Sheriff and let him know what's going on."

"The cell phones only work up on the ridge lines along here. The nearest one is a mile, maybe more."

Grant's breathing was deep, punctuated with grimaces every few exhalations. Something was wrong.

"Do you think the 911 call will get a response?" Grant asked as he struggled to stand.

"Probably, but it'll be at least an hour." In the dim light she could see a tear in his pants. He stood with most of his weight on the left leg. "You've been hit!"

He removed a bloodied hand from the hip of his fatigues. "I think it's a flesh wound … Not a lot of heavy bleeding anyway."

Crystal was amazed at his calm assessment. He'd seen a lot worse. "It needs to be dressed," she said, stating the obvious to the doctor.

"Not now. We need to get some distance between us and find a secure spot to watch for them." Grant looked up the slope and then back farther into the forest.

"A half-mile and we get to Blue Springs, the water is good. It's a storage site for boulders the Park Service has removed from the roads. The pines there keep the undergrowth down. Can you make it?"

"I'll make it. What did you get from the house?" he asked, pointing to a carrying case she'd rested against the tree.

"Just the shotgun. The .270 was locked up. Pretty sure I didn't have time to fool with that." She produced two boxes of shells from an oversized rain coat.

Grant grimaced and nodded. "Good work. We're gonna be giving up distance to them though … we can work with that."

He rose on a stiff leg. Crystal reached out to support him, her arm stretching around his firm, hard back. He accepted the assistance and gingerly pumped his right leg a few times.

"Should we go down to the springs? The ridge line is farther but the cell phone may work there," she said.

"They'd be expecting us to do something like that. We need them split up and to find a place we can defend." Grant hobbled lightly in a small circle, testing his leg. "Seems to be working okay. Let's go."

Crystal picked her way through the shrouded night, using her fully acclimated night vision to avoid black depressions in the forest floor and dark gray obstructions that were either bushes or boulders. Grant kept up well but was slowing as they reached the rock outcropping at the spring.

He picked an elevated spot that backed on the spring and shifted smaller stones to augment their protection. Trees grew right up to the outcropping. Scrub oaks and palmetto mixed with wire grass would make it hard moving through the underbrush.

"I think it's time to get you taken care of," Crystal said. "Let me get some water to clean that wound."

She unloaded the shells and shotgun next to Grant and slipped out of the coat. At the spring she rinsed the water-proof pockets and filled them with water. The coat had no lining. What would she use to clean Grant's wound? She didn't want to use her socks, they may have miles to walk yet. Besides, the socks were dirty. She tugged at the hem of her blouse but it resisted tearing and was a nylon base anyway. It was her underwear or brassiere.

She slipped out of her bra. One cup could be used for cleaning the wound, the other for a dressing. Would Grant appreciate the personal touch? And then the rain started, not heavy but a solid drizzle. Her wet top left little to the imagination. *Oh, hell!*

As she returned he actually did a double take, the second look lasting embarrassingly long. His face flushed as she explained, "The cleanest thing I had was my bra, and the wound needs cleaning. Sooo."

"You're right of course ... and I understand the sacrifice." He smirked, focusing on the delicate frilly garment.

As she arranged the dressings he repeatedly stole glances at her nearly exposed wet breasts. Her shameless pink areolae seemed to be on a mission of their own. Cautiously she eased down the waistline of his fatigues. Grant gripped the edge of his midnight blue jockey shorts modestly. By broken starlight she used the fresh water to clean the wound. It bled minimally. Some muscle was exposed but mostly it was a jagged skin laceration. She held pressure and what bleeding had begun soon stopped.

Using Grant's knife, she began to macerate some of the Devil's Shoestring roots from her pouch.

"What are you doing?" Grant asked as he surveyed the forest in front of their makeshift fortress.

"I'm preparing a dressing. The wound needs protection after it's cleaned."

"With roots?" he asked, leaning low to examine the mixture.

"The roots my grandpa asked me to bring to him. Normally I'd heat the paste but this will have to do."

Grant sat quietly.

"You don't want me using some old Indian treatment on you?"

"I didn't say that."

"Well, we don't have anything else. Your pack is still in the Jeep."

He resurveyed the approach to their stronghold, looked back at Crystal, and simply nodded.

"Right," Crystal said—mainstream medical people. If it wasn't taught in school, it must not be true. She bit her tongue. Now was not the time. She leaned forward and blew across the paste, blew the healing words into the potion as her grandfather, his mother, and her ancient ancestors had for thousands of years. It should have been done through a healing stick but hers were in the back of her grandfather's truck.

Holding the clean brassiere cup in washed hands, she lathered the paste thickly and secured the dressing with the bra strap. Finally she eased the pants back up his hip. He grimaced and made a hissing type sound through clenched teeth.

She crossed her legs and sat facing him. With hands extended to the sky, she softly chanted.

Grant watched her but did not interrupt. The chant was finished in less than three minutes. She sat quietly, contemplating.

"Is that it ... do I need to do something?" he asked.

Crystal tipped her head slightly. "My grandmother always said believing would help." She grinned. "Healing is a sacred pact between the plants of nature and the medicine person. There is more of course, spirituality—a firm connection with ancestors far back beyond known time."

Grant shifted his good leg and pushed further into the bunker. He nodded nearly imperceptibly.

She slipped the coat back on and pulled it snug against her breasts. That seemed to bother him as much as the dressing. "The Sheriff should be at the farm soon, if he got the message. He won't find much except your Jeep though. They won't know if we've been abducted or if we took off and which direction."

Grant motioned his head back up the wooded hill they'd come down. "The shooters will have split up to cover more ground. And they know they've only got a short time to get us." He wiped rain water from his soaked hair and eyebrows.

"Did you see how many there were?"

"Well, at least three." A hint of crow's feet framed hardened blue eyes. "Could be more ... maybe another vehicle."

Crystal crawled in next to him behind the wall of rocks. It was cramped, forcing them to lie across each other. She welcomed the warmth of his body. She hadn't been this close to a man in nearly two years, and that had proven to be just about as hopeless a situation as this.

"Thanks, the hip feels pretty good." Warm drops of rain dripped off his nose onto her cheek as he looked down on her. That and the close proximity of his tanned and handsome face produced a strangely pleasant reassurance.

"Their rifles probably have night vision and easily have a hundred yards or more range," Grant said. "But the rain may work to our benefit."

"Can't we wait them out?"

"Hopefully, but that won't be their plan. Once we're spotted they'll quickly converge and triangulate on us."

"It'll be hard for them to get behind us with the spring," Crystal said, trying to believe some reasonable chance for their survival existed.

"We don't want it to get to that."

"So what do you mean?"

"We need to lure them in one at a time and surprise them from a short distance. Probably no more than twenty yards, and that's a stretch for the shotgun," Grant said. "Which do you feel most confident with?"

She swallowed hard as his stone-cold face studied her. Kill another human being? She blinked back tears as her stomach churned. "Kill or be killed. That's what you're saying. You want us to lure them in and shoot them."

Eyebrow raised in assent, he reached out and squeezed her shoulder gently. "I'll be right here."

Crystal sniffed back the last onslaught of tears. "I'm good with a shotgun but not lying down and shooting to the side. I'd probably do better with the .45, if I can even shoot at another human."

"We need them to come right around the stone outcropping. It'll happen fast. You can't hesitate." Grant watched her wring her hands.

She honestly did not know how she would react when and if the time came. She nodded as confidently as she could. Neither of them was fooled.

Chapter 14

Blue Springs, Apalachicola National Forest

Grant had gathered a pile of stones he could use to draw the assassin in. The rustling of leaves would need to be investigated before a soldier would rally the others to his location. Many things in the forest rustled leaves.

Crystal's warm body nestled against his—slender curves with subtle, compliant muscles. Her breasts pressed against his abdomen as he scanned the tree line. Breasts he had glimpsed in stark relief, aroused by the rain and wind. Maybe a bit more by her anger at him over the wound treatment, but nonetheless aroused for his inspection. He hadn't meant to challenge her. It had all happened so quickly, he'd reacted poorly. Next time he resolved to approach it differently. "We'll mostly need to stay down behind the rocks, can't be looking around with their night-vision capabilities," Grant whispered.

She tilted her head slightly. Her eyes diverted down and to the right. A heightened response pose. She looked up and placed a finger on her lips.

Grant slid down the embankment ever-so-slightly and silently. He handed Crystal the .45. The shotgun was already loaded with three shells, one chambered. He released the safety but kept his finger off the trigger. She did the same.

Her head lifted slightly. He was about to urge her back down when her finger rose. She pointed to the right.

Grant shifted the shotgun and rolled slowly in that direction. He tossed a small stone off to the left, toward the bank of the spring. The sound was barely perceptible. Nothing moved. Except for the drumming of rain there was no sound, no thunder, and no assassin.

Crystal sat rigid, two hands on the pistol, concentrating on the forest. With her hands still on the .45, she wiggled her finger to the left.

Grant heard nothing. He hoped this was some Creek trait, a special sense of nature about her.

Her finger wagged now more urgently. Grant shifted back to his right to cover the left flank of the boulder pile. In doing so his elbow rested in her lower abdomen, indenting her jeans below the belt line. She gave him a quick glance and then refocused above the rock pile. Waiting, sensing. Rain-soaked hair clung to her cheeks.

Grant caught the quick deflection of her eyes to the left. She swiveled as a black-gloved hand and rifle barrel rounded the edge of the bolder. The rifle retorted just past her head three times. She shrunk back against Grant. The shotgun exploded. Grant rolled quickly from behind the boulders. The assassin fired, though more erratically. Grant glimpsed a shattered scope on the rifle as he fired the second shotgun blast. The assailant recoiled but did not drop. The repeated crack of the .45 came just behind his right ear. The flash burned against his cheek. The man staggered back two steps and collapsed.

Grant jumped on the man. He kicked the rifle toward the spring and knelt beside the crumpled assailant. Blood spurted from a neck wound. The man gurgled in agonal respirations. A bullet-proof vest showed signs of the shotgun blast and a least one .45 hollow point. All stopped by the vest. The lethal wound was a hollow point round to the soft vulnerable flesh of the neck. He stopped breathing.

Grant picked up the rifle and turned to Crystal. "Grab an arm. We need to drag the body behind the boulders before his buddies show up."

She stood with her left hand over her mouth.

"Crystal, honey ... come on, we don't have much time."

She stumbled over to Grant and holding the pistol in her right hand, pulled with her left, helping him drag the man behind the boulders.

Grant stripped off the bullet-proof vest, wiped it on the ground to remove most of the blood, and gave it to Crystal. "Put it on. We'll need all the luck we can get when his buddies show up."

In a near stupor she once again removed her coat, revealing glimpses of breasts that heaved with each breath. She slipped on the vest and turned as Grant secured the Velcro.

Once back in their bunker, Grant checked the rifle, which had several rounds left. He placed it next to the shotgun and eased the .45 from Crystal's shaking hand. He ensured the safeties were all engaged. Now they waited.

"He's dead?" Crystal asked.

"Yes." Grant didn't elaborate. She didn't need to know that her shot had killed the man —and saved their lives. Time for that later.

Chapter 15

Surgical Ward

Will woke with a start. He had out-slept his pain medication. Spasms shot up and down his leg, battling for supremacy. Earlier he'd struggled through a haze of medication to meet the eternal unseen power of nature, to regain the balance of wind, fire, water, and earth that would banish his suffering and bring harmony. Not tonight apparently. He grunted through the pain and reluctantly fumbled about for the nurse call button. Had he missed a call from Crystal? He sat up with his good leg off the bed, struggling to focus on the clock radio across the room, unable to turn completely because of the upper rail on the bed.

"Mr. Blackrock, please wait before you get up." An older, heavy set nurse came through the door wagging a finger at him, not Ashley. That meant it was the night shift and after seven o'clock.

Ignoring the reprimand he edged to the foot of the bed and let his good leg dangle. "Did my granddaughter call while I was asleep?"

"Sweetie, I have to tell you Ashley didn't mention that at our turnover. I'm Claris … the night shift, but you probably figured that out already." She smiled brightly and put both hands on her ample hips.

"What about the Sheriff? Did he call?" Will grimaced, trying to breath slowly and not let the pain take over. Ancient unwritten chants, in the Muscogee dialect, finally organizing in his mind.

"She didn't mention any calls. I'm sorry, Hon."

Claris stood before Will, blocking him from any attempt to stand on his own. It was not his intent anyway.

"Looks like you're due for some pain medication ... and by the look on your face, none too soon." She turned and waddled to the door. Gazing back over her shoulder, she said, "Don't you be trying anything stupid now, I'll be right back."

Where was Crystal? She knew to call, knew he'd be worried. Had a call just been missed? No, he could sense that more was going on. Certainly she should be safe with the Sheriff and Doctor Sands. It couldn't have taken them this long to get out to the river and back, especially with the four-wheelers.

Claris returned with two pills. She filled his glass with water and waited for him to take them.

"I need to contact my granddaughter," Will said.

The nurse snorted, pulled the phone off the bedside stand, and handed it to Will. "Dial nine for an outside line. You're gonna need to take those pain pills though. The pain is just going to get worse. Your last dose was nearly six hours ago."

He nodded. "As soon as I get through to her."

She rolled her eyes.

"I'll be asleep half hour after I take these." Will shook the pills in his hand. "Do I need both of them?"

"One's a muscle relaxant, the other a pain pill. You're gonna need them both tonight, trust me."

"Great, I'll be out until morning."

"If you don't take 'em you'll be up all night in pain. But hey, it's your funeral, bub." With that the compassionate beef of a woman swung her generous hips and lumbered out of the room.

Will punched nine followed by Crystal's cell number. The tone went immediately to message saying the member was not available for service. He hoped that didn't mean they were still out in the national forest, outside of cell range. Why would they still be? He left a message for her to call and that he was worried. Then just on a lark he tried the Blackrock farm in case she'd stopped there for a change of clothes or something. After seven rings the answering machine picked-up. He left a similar message. Where was she?

Murderers on the river, Crystal struggling with death and evil, himself confined to a modern super-sterile institution far from the forest. Any attempt at harmony tonight would sap what strength he had left. Reluctantly he swallowed the two pills and debated calling the Sheriff but it was too early to call out the Mounted Police. Besides, if it was something innocent, Crystal would be furious that he'd involved the authorities. Maybe the debonair doctor had her secreted away for a nice dinner. He didn't really believe that. The drugs were clouding his reasoning. And there was something else just beyond his consciousness, something about the doctor that pulled at Will. Through an ever thickening haze he decided to try all the calls again, when he woke up.

The aroma of cedar and sage, visions of eagle feathers and ancient chants swirled in his head as he lay back and pulled the covers over his head, blotting out the light from the parking lot. Then, all thoughts of the sacred path left his mind as the medicine overtook him.

Chapter 16

Blue Springs

The cold that gripped Crystal was more than just the late-summer chill of the forest. Death lay at her feet. The realization that, but for fractions of seconds, it could be her lifeless body lying grotesquely among the rocks. The fragility of life and the unabashed brutality left her drained and naked.

Grant pulled her in closely to him. "You did what you had to do, Crystal."

Tears rolled down her face. She'd killed animals before, but that was a sacred bond between her and nature. A process by which nutrition and substance was transferred—respectfully and with appreciation to the animal giving up its life. This was mindless and evil.

She had seen the results of violent deaths, but had never been the instrument of that death. This was horrible. She shuddered uncontrollably.

Grant's arms held her. Strong warm hands cupped her shoulders and restrained the spasms. "Breathe slowly," he said. "It will pass."

Oh my God! This was what he suffered through in combat. Had anyone been there to hold him as he convulsed and shook? Surely not. Crystal buried her head in his shoulder. The tears flowed helplessly. And then slowly, the shaking stopped. The warmth of his body engulfed her—her heart ached in concert with his. She simultaneously experienced grief, sorrow, relief, and a strange sense of belonging.

His head rested on hers. She was unsure if the rain continued to drip from him or if he also was crying. She did not look up.

◆

It had taken nearly a half hour for Crystal to settle. Grant struggled to maintain some semblance of alertness as he comforted the distraught woman. Near the end, he discerned a cricket click far off to the south that may have been answered to the west. He hadn't picked up on the cadence or sequence but he was certain it was the assassins. A coded response was expected from their man. What the consequences of a missed check would bring, Grant had no idea.

"Are they coming?" Crystal whispered as she rolled in close to Grant.

"I think they're far off still," he answered.

"Will they come?"

"I don't know. They know that their associate isn't answering their calls to him."

"How do you know that?"

"Cricket clicks. I heard them about ten minutes ago, pretty far off."

"Cricket clicks?"

"Yeah, not very sophisticated." Rain drops dripped from his hair as he tilted his head. "Especially with all the night-vision stuff. I guess it could have been a backup in case they lost their main source of communication. I didn't hear any radio on our man though—might have been some other system."

"Sorry I lost it there." She reached over, retrieved the .45, and checked the safety.

"You were great, saved the day."

Her hands were no longer shaking.

As the rain picked up, Grant rigged her coat above them as a sort of tent. He kept his head positioned to hear any approach, but he hadn't heard the first man. Only Crystal had known where he was and when he would appear—even in the rain. At first Grant had thought she was listening, but near the end it was her innate ability to just know where the man was, and how close.

"We'll need to stay alert," Grant said, but what he really meant was that they needed Crystal to use whatever her power was to warn them of approaching danger.

"I think they're still a ways away," Crystal said in a hushed tone.

"Did you hear him coming?" Grant asked.

She raised an eyebrow to him. "Something like that."

She was not going to launch into some new Creek lore/Caucasian controversy. Accept it for what it was, he told himself. What would it be like in a different situation to be lying with Crystal Blackrock in his arms, to have her willingly come to him seeking refuge and intimacy? He stared at her shapely body that nestled so naturally against his, petite and vulnerable.

"The Sheriff should've been to the farm by now," Crystal said. "But I haven't heard any sirens. I think we would have."

"They might have come with sirens muted," Grant said.

"We could only hope."

"The longer we go, the better our odds," he said, quietly dumping water from the coat.

"Did he have a radio or anything?" Crystal asked.

"Not that I saw." Grant rolled next to the dead assassin and inspected the body. When he turned back he held an earpiece with an electric wire and battery pack. He held the receiver to his ear. Nothing.

"They probably know their communications are compromised," he said. "The only night vision this one had was the scope on the rifle.

"Now what?" Crystal adjusted the bullet-proof vest and studied Grant while he scanned the bunker.

"We wait. Time is on our side, so we use what gives us an advantage." Grant settled back into their den, adjusting a few rocks here and there.

•

She shivered. They were animals, huddled in their den, their lair. Waiting for what would happen next, being reactive, not proactive. This was what war was like. Using whatever advantage you had to survive. Not making the wrong decision. The first assassin had made the wrong decision. The others stayed out in the wet forest scheming and planning. What did they consider their most useful assets? They had the superior weapons. Or at least thought they did. Now they weren't sure. Originally they outnumbered her and Grant but that had been evened up. They were ruthless, but apparently Grant could be also. Despite the precariousness of the predicament, the current situation was a stalemate. And as Grant had mentioned, time was on their side.

"I think they'll leave," she said.

Grant glanced at her and smiled warily. "You could be right. But what we don't know is what price they'll pay for failure. It could be worse than being gunned down by us or the Sheriff."

"What could be worse than that?"

"Having your family tortured. Sisters and wives raped. Parents executed."

Crystal felt the pang of remorse mixed with anger. It was Grant's. "Is that what happens in Afghanistan?"

"Some of it … They use whatever they can to make the men and young boys fight." Grant looked away, unwilling to hold her eyes. There was more to this. "It's a different society over there … very different." Grant rolled a stone over and over in his hand.

He would not say more on his own, but he needed to. This Crystal knew, as she usually knew things about people. She hesitated to say more, but what the hell, could she really make the situation worse? "Our Afghan allies could also be brutal, weren't they?" she asked in a low, she hoped non-threatening, voice.

He did not answer.

"Our military, our society, expects soldiers to suffer these atrocities on their own for the most part. That's true, isn't it? It's only the ones who complain, the ones who break, those diagnosed with post traumatic stress disorder that actually get the treatment they need."

Still he said nothing.

She sensed it. She knew. *Doctor, heal thyself.* That was what Grant Sands had suffered these past years. He was not diagnosed with post traumatic stress disorder, he had not broken in the true sense, and he was not a complainer. He was strong, intelligent, and disciplined. And he was his own worst enemy. He probably could go on for years, maybe his entire life, living in a shell. Keeping the rest of the world out, preventing the world —preventing a woman —from seeing the turmoil that broiled inside.

But he couldn't keep out Crystal Blackrock.

Chapter 17

Blue Springs

The night wore on. The rain stopped and the clouds cleared. But then the temperature dropped. The fine mist of his breath hung between the improvised roof and their heads. It would be best if they waited until the morning, unless the Sheriff or other law enforcement showed up. He'd been pinned down before, more than once. The plan had always been to hunker down and wait for reinforcements. Grant saw no reason to deviate from that scenario, except for the probing of Crystal.

No doubt she saw right into his soul, his mind, his very being. He had felt her heartache after the attack. But it was more than that. It was a shared ache, as intimate as any lovemaking or personal bond he had ever experienced. How had this happened? There was no rational physiological explanation. All his training and education failed him. And he was being drawn to this woman in ways he did not understand.

"It should be light soon." His watch read 5:40. "It would probably be best to move to a ridge line away from the house—"

"One with a forest-road access so we can contact the Sheriff and hopefully avoid the other assailants," Crystal finished for him.

"Right, which way would that be?"

"If we move to the southeast ... about a mile, mile and a half at the most, we'll be at Cooper's Ridge. I know cell phones work there and they can get to us off county route 220."

"Let's give it another thirty minutes or so." He stretched his legs. The right one pulled at the hip but eventually began to loosen up.

"You gonna be okay for that distance?"

He began an improvised morning stretch sequence. His inclination was to declare forcefully that it would be no problem. But it might be. And Crystal would know that. "I'll give it my best. If I can't make it all the way, you'll need to get to the ridge and make the call."

She sized him up, chuckling. "I'm not going to carry you up hill. That's for sure." Her face beamed. She had recovered miraculously from the previous night's attack.

"I'm glad it's me and not you that got hit last night."

"Yeah … you wouldn't be pulling my pants down to do any doctoring." The faintest of sparkles danced in her eyes. "I know, I know. 'Trust me, I'm a doctor.'"

They both laughed.

"I have very gentle hands I'll have you know," he countered.

"I bet. Is that what all the nurses say?"

"Hey, you're impugning my reputation." Grant feigned a hurt expression.

"Yeah, right bud."

Her whimsical smile lightened Grant's spirit. She was beautiful, even in her smudged clothing, bulletproof vest, and wet stringy hair.

Then the sparkle was gone. Her stern gaze focused behind him on the ground and brought him back to the urgency of their situation.

Rain had washed most of the blood from the dead attacker leaving a pale, creamy complexion. There was nothing to be done with the man until the authorities could be led back to the spring. In the emerging light, he appeared middle aged and probably of Hispanic descent.

Crystal would not look at the body. She sat and readjusted the large, awkward vest.

"Is it too heavy?" Grant asked, pointing to the vest.

"Do you think I really need to wear it?"

"Probably … but it wouldn't stop one of their high-velocity rounds. I don't know." Grant shrugged.

•

Ultimately Crystal decided to leave the oversized vest with the dead attacker. With the pistol in one hand, she used the other to help Grant over fallen trees and up the leaf and mold covered slopes.

Fog hung over the forest as they trudged toward the glow of the morning sun. Crystal skirted a shallow creek at the bottom of a ravine, checking for slippery spots before waving Grant across. Pines quickly gave way to scrub oaks and hickory with the occasional dogwood. The underbrush was sparse, mainly tree litter, dollar leaf, and beggar weeds. They made good time though Grant did grunt and stumble on several occasions.

"That's the ridge line. It's about two hundred feet to the top." Crystal pointed to a distant elevation where the sun was just beginning to peek above the outcropping.

Grant did one last survey behind them and toward the low areas approaching Cooper's Ridge. "This is the dangerous part," he said. "If they're still around, they'll expect us to try and get to higher ground or back to the Jeep. If they start shooting, fire the .45 in the general direction. That'll give me a chance to get the rifle on them." He handed Crystal the shotgun case. "You need to be in position halfway up by that fallen pine." He pointed midway up the scrub-covered hill and then swung a nearly two-hundred-seventy-degree arc, taking in all the potential hiding places for the assassins.

"That should give you some protection too, assuming they're not split up. If that's the case, I'll take the one who's looking into the sun first. So you should fire at the other one and get around the other side of the tree. Does that make sense?"

"Sure, but I don't think they're anywhere near here," Crystal said. He was taking smart precautions, but the balance of nature in this part of the forest was in harmony. There were no evil or dark forces at work on this glorious morning. Squirrels scampered here and there, an occasional cotton mouse and some bobwhite quail. She sensed nothing else. The squeal and feather flapping of the quail though had given them both a start, more Grant than her.

Grant began the climb. A small amount of fresh blood spotted his fatigues. Hopefully they could get that taken care of soon. She continuously scanned the low areas to the right and left of the ridgeline as Grant had done. If the assassins were up above, Grant would spot them first.

He made good time, silently moving up the fairly gentle rise. Soon he disappeared behind a grouping of scrub oaks. Crystal waited, her palms sweaty on the pistol. It seemed a long time. What would she do if something happened to him up on the ridge? She'd have to go back down and further into the forest. That was all she could do. She'd be fine in the forest. She'd spent many days there and knew how to survive, quite comfortably actually. Maybe they should have done that in the first place.

Grant waved the rifle above his head and gestured for her to join him on the ridge. With the gun in her right hand and the shotgun case under her left arm, she picked her way up the slope, relief clearing the tightness in her chest and steadying her hands.

Grant knelt as she approached, surveying the ravines for any movement. "It looks clear," he said. "We do have a signal. What do I tell them about where we are?"

"Just tell Sheriff Tumley we're on Cooper's Ridge above Blackrock Ravine. He'll know how to get here."

"Really, the ravine we just came up is called Blackrock Ravine?"

"Yeah, and this would be Blackrock Ridge if it wasn't for some European guy with survey equipment."

He pointed to his head with the thumb up and then dropped the hammer.

"Sit down and let me look at that hip. It's bleeding again."

Grant sat and eased down his fatigues slightly while raising his shirt. Six pack abdominals, of course. Crystal unconsciously licked her lips and caught herself halfway through the motion. It took extreme control to concentrate on the soaked brassiere remnant.

Luckily only the bottom of the dressing was bloody. She rolled the pants back in position and held pressure as she watched the muscles of Grant's stomach contract and move with his breathing.

"Not too bad," Grant said without wincing. As she repositioned her hands every few minutes, he relaxed his head on his elbow, and closed his eyes.

Would he really look that innocent when he slept?

As it turned out, the Sheriff and several of his deputies were at the Blackrock farm and had been there most of the night. They drove up to the overlook at Cooper's Ridge not ten minutes after Grant called.

Chapter 18

Cooper's Ridge

As soon as they arrived the Sheriff sent his men, complete with communication ear-phones, rifles, and flak jackets, down both sides of the ridge to do a formal sweep of the area. Crystal marveled at how clean and pressed Tumley's uniform was despite a night of work.

The Sheriff asked Grant if he needed an ambulance. Grant declined.

"We swept most of the forest roads north and east of the farm last night but found no one," Sheriff Tumley said. "You two look like drowned rats."

"Thanks," Crystal said, brushing hair from her eyes and pulling the coat tight about her breasts. At least she was holding up better than Grant. "It was not my most comfortable camping night, I'll tell you that. If you've got a first-aid kit, that wound on his hip could use a change of dressing and some antiseptic."

"I'll have Scott look at it as soon as they get back up," the Sheriff said as he surveyed the area, rifle at the ready. "That one of their rifles?"

Grant retracted the breech of the weapon, handed the rifle to Tumley, and bent gingerly to pick up the unspent cartridge that had ejected.

"An AK-47, I'll be damned. You guys ran in to some tough cookies. Down along the border with Mexico these guys just kill whoever they think might cooperate with the police." The Sheriff looked over the mist-covered hills of the gloomy dawn. "Sends a message." Grant explained the happenings of the night to Sheriff Tumley as one of the deputies retrieved the first-aid kit.

"So one of them is dead down behind the rock pile at Blue Springs?" The Sheriff looked at Crystal and then to Grant. "We never heard any shots. I guess we got to the farm after all that had happened." He picked his hat off his head and rubbed a hand through a smattering of grey hair before replacing the hat. "I'm sure sorry, if we had heard shots, we'd have come down into the forest last night. We wouldn't have waited."

Grant waved a dismissive hand at Tumley. "Hey, I understand, Sheriff. You can only act on the information and intel you have. We all did the best we could."

The Sheriff stepped back, observing Grant. "Iraq or Afghanistan?"

"Afghanistan."

The Sheriff pulled down the brim of his hat and looked out toward the struggling sun. He inhaled deeply and slowly exhaled through his nose. His thoughts probably mired in some far way foreign battle field.

How could this be happening in the Panhandle of Florida? Heat rose in Crystal's neck and cheeks.

Grant nodded, but his long face also showed the inhumanity of war. She held Grant's arm. He turned with a twitch, clear eyes fixed her gaze, then lowered to her lips. She moistened them with her tongue and smiled.

"Does my grandfather know anything about this? Has anyone contacted him?" Crystal asked the Sheriff, interrupting the awkward moment.

"No. I really didn't want to talk with anyone until I knew what was goin' on," Sheriff Tumley answered. A tight set to his lips replaced his gloomy expression.

"Here, use my cell phone to call him," Grant said, handing the phone to Crystal. "I'm sure he's worried, not having heard from you last night."

She had to ask Grant for the number to the hospital and go through the operator before the phone rang in her grandfather's room. It was picked up on the second ring.

"Grandpa, it's Crystal."

"Oh, child you have given me a frightful night."

"I'm fine, Grandpa. We stopped at the farm to pick up some

things and ran into a little trouble, but everything is okay now." She shifted her stance and looked up at Grant.

"I tried to reach you last night and talked to the Sheriff's office this morning. Is he out there with you?"

"He is. I'll tell you about it when we get back to town. But we are all just fine. You be careful too. These guys mean business, not too happy to have us poking our noses around apparently." Grant limped around one of the SUVs with a deputy and sat on the tailgate.

"This isn't your fight, Crystal," her grandfather said. "Let the Sheriff and FBI take care of running them down."

"I couldn't agree more, Grandpa. And I'm sure Doctor Sands feels the same way, but I'll tell you more after I get some food and clean up … You rest some now, okay?"

"I'll try. I feel like a prisoner though. I think I ran into the head guard last night." He chuckled.

"Hang in there, Grandpa. Love ya … see you soon."

Crystal pushed end, closed her eyes briefly, and held the phone against her forehead. The tightness in her shoulders eased. She stood for a moment and breathed deeply, watching the sun burn off the early morning haze.

The deputy was holding her dismantled bra when she walked around the side of the Sheriff's vehicle.

"That's not a souvenir for you, Deputy," Crystal said as she snatched the torn lingerie and stuffed it into her coat pocket.

Both men looked like children who'd lost their candy.

The deputy scowled. "Looks like you got further with her than any of us have, Doc."

Crystal kicked him in the shin.

"Hey!" he yelled. Then he turned to Grant. "Are you sure it wasn't her that shot you?"

"Keep it up, Scott, and I'll be talking to your big sister … again." Crystal smirked at the deputy.

He turned back to Grant, face flushed. "Looks pretty good," he said as he withdrew the root paste and dressing.

"Sure does," Grant said. He scrunched his mouth and nodded to Crystal.

"I think the good doctor can direct you in what it needs next, Scott." Crystal pirouetted smartly and walked back to talk with the

Sheriff.

Grant needed his wound formally cleaned and stitched. They positioned him in the front of the Sheriff's SUV and Crystal climbed into the back. The drive, on switchback roads, to the Blackrock farm bounced Grant mercilessly. A spasm gripped Crystal's right hip every time she saw him grimace. Once at the farm, Tumley decided that Grant would ride back to town with Crystal driving his Jeep. Two of the deputies would follow them to the emergency room.

"I think the assailants are long gone," the Sheriff said as Crystal returned with Scott and her overnight bag from the farm house. "Probably pulling up and heading somewhere else."

"That does all make sense," Grant said. "But why in the Hell would they be coming out here after Crystal?" His face was flush as he confronted the Sheriff.

The two looked like stags about to face off. There was something she was missing. She put a hand on Grants chest. "Whoa, partner. What is this all about?"

"Well, there's more to it, I'm afraid," Sheriff Tumley said as he stood next to the Jeep. He spit a cheek-full of tobacco into a drainage ditch and squinted into the sun as it broke above the trees. "The FBI will be wanting to talk with the two of you, and probably your grandfather."

Crystal frowned. "Really, the FBI?"

"Yeah, they've got an axe to grind I'm afraid." The Sheriff scratched under his eye while Grant glared down on him. "I think we've got our own problem though."

Grant eased himself up into the Jeep's passenger seat. "Let's have the FBI's side first if you don't mind."

The Sheriff sighed and nodded. Apparently he felt more at ease talking about the FBI's interests more than his own.

"Trafficking, I suspect," the Sheriff said. "They've never been real forthcoming with us locals. Claims there are national security issues." He kicked dirt on the snuff he had spit. "I'll set your meeting up for tomorrow morning," he added.

Crystal stood with her foot on the running-board, head tipped slightly. "Does this have to do with the 'mostly' you talked about at the river?"

"Ma'am ... " Tumley diverted his gaze from hers. "You didn't hear any of this from me." He glanced to make sure his men were out of earshot. "Some of the bodies we've found were dismembered." He looked from Crystal to Grant, scowling. ". . . And sometimes we just found discarded clothes ... women's clothes mostly."

"Great," Grant shook his head and mumbled.

"Women's clothing ... not the women, just clothing? What kind of trafficking are you talking about, Sheriff?" Crystal narrowed her eyes at Tumley.

The Sheriff shifted his gaze to Grant.

"Human traffickers, I'm afraid," Grant said.

"You mean sex slaves and all?" A lump formed in Crystal's throat.

"And more, I'm afraid, Miss Blackrock," the Sheriff said. "... not pretty."

Crystal raised her eyebrows.

"They're smugglers basically, except these guys don't stop at drugs." The Sheriff took off his hat and mopped his forehead with a dirty handkerchief. "They'll move anything they can buy cheap, steal, or kidnap—as long as they can get top dollar for it somewhere."

"And your other concern is there must be a local connection," Grant said. "To keep them around and after Crystal and Will, right?"

"The forest is remote, but there is activity at certain times of the year." Tumley pinched a chew of tobacco from a Skoal bag and slid it into his left cheek. "And the roads in and out are poorly marked ... somebody knows the area ... I'd bet someone local."

"That's why they wanted to clean up loose ends," Crystal finished for him. "Do you think grandpa or I might be able to identify them?"

"We certainly can't rule that out," Tumley shook his head.

"Do you think they'll try again?" Crystal was standing now hands on hips.

"They'd have to be crazy," Tumley chewed slowly. "But I can't predict what their next move would be ... best to be prepared."

The other deputy, Cross, had rejoined the group. He nodded. "You all were lucky. These guys don't usually come up empty handed."

The Sheriff tipped his hat. "Sorry about this folks. We best get back to town and try to sort this all out," he said and turned to his SUV.

In the Jeep, Grant sat balancing his weight on the left side, shaking his head in disgust and frustration. "So, after being up all night and shot, I get to talk to the FBI ... I've been told I needed to get a life. I don't think this is what they meant."

Crystal climbed in and adjusted the driver's seat, pushed on the clutch pedal, and tested the gear shift. "Do you think one or more of the smugglers knows grandpa or me?"

"You all spend a lot of time out here and in the forest. Makes sense if this person knows the river and roads like your grandfather and you ... You may have run across them, maybe even had some dealings with them."

Her knuckles whitened on the steering wheel, stomach muscles tightened as she fought an urge to jump from the Jeep and run. Run where? She alone knew hundreds of people from local farmers, to medical personnel, park rangers, and numerous shop and convenience store workers. Her grandfather knew everyone in the area basically.

"This is impossible!" Crystal breathed deeply and shook her head. "It could be anybody."

Grant made a sipping sound between clenched teeth as he shifted around to face Crystal. "Look, this is a job for the Sheriff. And there are some assumptions that could be reasonably made."

Tension eased from Crystal's neck, hands, and abdomen. She exhaled slowly and released the clutch, following Sheriff Tumley and the deputies out of the Blackrock compound.

"Could be more than one of them though," she said.

"I was thinking they'd have to have to own a four-wheel drive to get through some of those forest roads."

"Yeah, and that really limits the prospects here in the Panhandle." Crystal chuckled.

"Good point." Grant repositioned his injured leg.

Crystal breathed deeply exhaling through pursed lips. Sunlight streamed in through the driver's side window and the dust abated as they turned onto the paved road, passing the spot where her mother had the accident. The leather smell and firm mechanics of the Jeep thankfully eased the sour taste in her mouth.

"I could use some coffee and maybe a sausage biscuit on the

way to town," Grant said.

Crystal rubbed cream over her dry hands and tossed a small tub of ginger body butter to Grant. He stared back with puffy eyes and tousled hair. "Miller's, just when we get on Route 22, the best biscuits in the panhandle. I'm sure the escorts would be good with that." She smiled. "Shouldn't you be keeping your stomach empty?"

"This won't require surgery, just some cleaning in the ER."

"Well, at least you won't have to explain the brassiere bandage."

"I owe you for that," Grant said. "Was that Victoria's Secret and what size replacement bra do I need to buy for you?"

"No way, bub … good try though. Your fraternity buddies would be proud of you."

Grant smirked. "Coffee," he bleated.

The lack of sleep had made Grant a little punch drunk, his college-kid antics being just a lame attempt at flirting. She'd had plenty of passes directed her way over the last few years but none from the likes of Doctor Grant Sands. He surely wouldn't be so loose lipped once he had some coffee in him.

Under different circumstances would he even give her the time of day? Really, they'd been pretty much forced together these past two days —and tomorrow looked as if it had also been planned out. She was relieved Grant would be with her when she talked to the FBI. What would they want? And who in the Panhandle could be working with human traffickers?

Chapter 19

The emergency room had the faint, stale odor of a busy previous night accentuated by pungent antiseptic. Crystal was unsure which smell she liked the least. Overflowing trash cans stood in contrast to a largely empty waiting room composed of rows of metal chairs covered in green vinyl. The treatment area, where Grant sat perched on a pillow-less gurney, was for the most part deserted. Except for a nurse and doctor whom he seemed to know personally. They talked in clipped medical and trauma terms that she understood intermittently. With a brief wave, she left Grant in their care.

In the rest room mirror her reflection was that of a disheveled homeless lady. The trip to the bathroom at Miller's Roadside Café had done little to improve the impression. She left with a rubber band holding her hair in a long ponytail and wet smudge marks where dirt had previously graced her jacket and pants. Time to confront her grandfather.

He sat on the bed reading, sections of newspaper spread everywhere within easy reach. His good leg swung back and forth as if he were casually exercising.

"Granddaughter, you are a sight for sore eyes." He hugged her, and then held her at arm's length. "Haven't they let you shower and change yet?"

Crystal tugged at her soiled and wrinkled T-shirt. "We just got in." She struggled not to cry as the emotions of the previous night welled up inside her. Here, in front of her grandfather, she had always laid her fears, frustrations, and failures. His arms had been her sanctuary since before she could remember. But some problems Grandpa could not solve, wouldn't try, and tears were not the answer.

"Sit next to me, child."

She was unable to hide her distress. Already she could see the burden her problems were putting on his heart and soul. They sat next to each other in silence.

Crystal respected the quiet. Her grandfather would call upon the sacred unseen powers of the Creek to bring her back to harmony. Certainly she needed to do things for herself, but those activities and actions outside of her control were the purview of the Creator. Solutions would come in time through the earthly elements, as they always did.

Finally he turned to her. "What happened last night?"

Crystal told him every detail with calm detachment, as was expected of a Creek medicine person. She did not tell him of her attraction to Grant Sands. That she could have such feelings for a non-Indian still baffled her. Certainly they had been bound together in the fire of conflict and danger. But there was more, an uncanny or mysterious connection that should not exist.

Was it his pure masculinity? The taut muscles she had seen and felt through the previous night? A chiseled body she craved to have next to her—on top of her—naked. She tore her thoughts back to the present.

Her grandfather scrutinized her as he sipped coffee from the metal cup he had packed into the forest with them. "You said they think these men are traffickers. What does that mean?"

"I guess they smuggle just about anything, including humans, girls mostly. It is really disgusting. The Sheriff said we'd need to talk to the FBI. You too, Grandpa."

"It doesn't make sense … What could they want from us now?" Normally vibrant, her grandfather visibly wore his age today.

"Grant and the Sheriff think they have a local accomplice."

"Someone from Panama City?" Her grandfather stepped back, head tilted.

"Well, someone familiar with the National Forest … and yes, maybe the area in general," she said.

Her grandfather nodded. "And they may know us. Is that what they're thinking?"

"I'm afraid so, Grandpa."

"I can't believe that ... here in the Panhandle?" His head shook with disappointment.

Crystal held his hands. "We just have to be careful and keep our eyes open, Grandpa." She tried her best to smile. "Have they given you an idea when you should be able to leave?"

"Forty-eight to seventy-two hours of antibiotics in the veins." Her grandfather pointed to two plastic bags with yellow and green labels hanging from a metal pole. "The surgeon, Doctor McAlister or something, said now is the time to get ahead of any infection, not after it's set up."

"Is it likely to get infected?"

"No. I treated the wounds well, waiting for you and the Sheriff to get back out on the trail."

"Are the antibiotics just a backup then ... Do you really need them?"

"It could need more surgery." Her grandfather pulled his lower lip and shrugged. "The doctor would be very angry if I refused his antibiotics and then he had to re-operate ... Modern medicine."

"Makes sense, I guess." Crystal rose and retrieved her backpack. "I brought the haloneske from your root cellar. We didn't have a chance yesterday to look for fresh roots. These worked well on Doctor Sands' wound though."

"He let you dress his wound?" He smirked and folded the newspapers sitting on his bed.

"There was nothing else to use." Crystal left out the part about using her brassiere. "It took a little convincing."

"Still, for a doctor to let you do that." He smiled. "I think he's soft on you."

Crystal turned from her elder so he would not see the flush that rose in her cheeks. This was where a girl needed her mother. Discussions about men had always been strained between Crystal and her grandfather. Not from his standpoint. He frequently asked her about boys or men she had dated—about what she liked in them, their strengths, and their weaknesses. She, on the other hand, had always been restrained. Not that his advice was anything but compassionate and insightful. But Crystal always felt he was interviewing men to be sperm donors for his great-grandchildren.

"It's not like that, Grandpa. It can't be." What Crystal didn't say was that non-Indian blood would dilute and compromise the progression of their Creek heritage.

Her grandfather reached for her hand. "You're worried about his roots. It is a concern ... But the true measure is can he find harmony with nature, and ultimately connect with the Sacred Way?"

"He's a prep-school kid from Atlanta, Grandpa ... " Crystal turned back. The flush gone, replaced by a spirited rebuttal, a common occurrence in the Blackrock house these past few years.

Her grandfather raised a leathery worn palm. "Again, my child, our search is for oneness with the universe. Do you think our relatives who have intermarried with the Cherokees, Shawnees, Seminole, and even Europeans are incapable of attaining harmony?"

Crystal sat dumbfounded. This was a side of her grandfather she had never seen. "What about our clan—the passing of our healing ways—the selection of the next medicine person? Our ability to meet and join with the unseen powers could be lost?"

"That is always a possibility." He stretched his arms wide. "World history is full of such misfortune. But it's also full of stories of rebirth. Not just in the Creek and other tribes but in natives from Africa, even some European societies."

"But they are so different from us, Grandpa. Our ancestors didn't even know of their existence." The pit of her stomach liquefied like melted butter. Her thoughts raced through her high school years, the medical clinic, Grandmother Blackrock, and her own personal battle to connect with her ancient relatives.

"They are different. But the ones who are able to reach harmony with the unseen powers have much more in common with us than differences."

"Perhaps I will understand better some day. I hope I have the strength and patience to see what you speak of," Crystal said. What she didn't say, what had hung over her for several years, was the nagging self-doubt. Modern-day materialism and society pulled at her and interfered daily with her, mostly fruitless attempts to find a balance—a harmony—with her gift.

"Whoever you choose," her grandfather said, "will be a member of the Wind Clan ... it is the heart of our culture. The maternal line sustained. Trust that the Creator has a divine reason to preserve Creek heritage."

"Would you have ever considered marriage outside the tribe?

To a non-Indian?" She swiped her tongue about her mouth to relieve the dryness.

"I didn't have to think about it. Your grandmother chose me. I didn't know it at first. And I'm sure she sweated it out awhile. But eventually it all worked out." He smiled and laughed.

"I just don't know, Grandpa. But I have to tell you the pickings for a thirty-two-year-old in our local tribe are pretty slim." She joined him in laughter. "All the good ones were taken years ago."

Chapter 20

Community Medical Emergency Room

Grant examined the neat row of stitches along his right hip.

"Pretty clean wound," Jake Robinson, the emergency-room physician commented. "I'm just gonna make a note here that this has already been reported to the police, right?" He held a clipboard with a multi-page official-looking form that he quickly checked through.

"Yeah, in fact you can confirm that with the deputy who just walked in," Grant said.

"Doctor." Deputy Scott Lang shook hands with Robinson. "We've filed the report already. Can I speak with Doctor Sands?"

"Sure, we're pretty much done here. I'll have the nurse put a dressing on for you." Robinson disappeared into another patient cubicle.

"Sheriff Tumley's confirmed your appointment at the federal building tomorrow with Agent Sandra Meyers. Eleven o'clock okay?"

"Fine," Grant said. What choice did he really have? "That'll give me a chance to clean up after my shift. Now I need to get home, catch a few hours sleep before this evening." He needed some rest. Maybe Tim Byron could catch evening rounds for him.

"That was the other thing Sheriff Tumley asked me to talk with you about."

"What?" Grant said, frowning.

"It would make a big difference," Deputy Lang said, "If we could some how watch both you and Miss Blackrock with one deputy at a time."

"And how do you propose to do that?"

"The department can't afford to put both of you up at a hotel. And we really don't want to inconvenience you anymore."

"So, what are you getting at? Having Miss Blackrock stay at my townhouse?"

The deputy grimaced and focused on the nurse as she entered the room.

Grant felt nothing of the bandaging procedure as he stewed about the Sheriff's lame plan. With the dressing in place, Grant stood and tested his leg and hip. A little stiff, but overall not bad for having been shot and lying in the forest all night.

As the nurse left, Deputy Lang cocked his shoulders back and hooked his thumbs in his belt. "She's a handful, that Crystal Blackrock. Some of us from the football team in high school attended a green corn ceremony where Crystal and her grandfather had arranged the stomp-dance grounds …"

"So she works with her grandfather doing his medicine work?" Grant asked.

"Actually, I think she's an initiated medicine woman herself. Though I don't know of her ever doing any healings or ceremonies on her own."

"So the stomp dance is a sacred ritual?"

"Right … yeah … it's part of the green corn celebration, promoting harmony with nature." He looked out of the cubicle to see if anyone was in ear shot. "Some of us were screwing around with the deer's tongue. In the ceremony, it represents the contribution of animals to Creek life. Crystal really tore into us. I'd never seen her that angry."

"That's what got between the two of you?"

"No." He chuckled. "That just started it. She told my older sister, who for the next five years was on my case about respecting Creek ceremonies and nature."

"Oh, hence the big-sister comment."

"It's not really like that though. Crystal and I actually dated a few years back." He looked into the cowboy hat in his hand. "She's a tough cookie. Probably make someone a good wife one day if they can break her." He smiled and kicked Grant in his good foot.

"I don't think I have spurs big enough for that job." Grant laughed but also visualized Crystal's shapely ass and briefly pictured himself trying to ride her. Shaking his head, he rose and gingerly flexed his hip up and down. Tension on the stitches stung a little. "Does the Sheriff really think he can talk her into staying at my place?"

"He was leaving that job to you."

"Great!"

"From what I hear, you live in an enclosed community on a dead-end street that backs on the water, should be a reasonable stake out."

"Yeah, I bet," Grant said, rolling his eyes.

•

The receptionist told Crystal that Doctor Sands and the Sheriff's deputy were in the triage checkout area. She rounded the corner to find them head to head, deep in conversation.

"Crystal," Deputy Lang said.

"Scott." Crystal's smile faded as Grant turned, shaking his head. "What's the matter?"

"Nothing," the deputy answered, turning to Grant.

Grant nervously massaged his two-day growth of beard then looked from the deputy back to Crystal, raised an eyebrow, and pointed down the hallway to a snack bar. "Why don't we get a cup of coffee while Deputy Lang finishes up his paperwork?"

Crystal normally limited her morning coffee. Not today. Sitting facing each other, she watched Grant play with the plastic stir stick. "How's the leg?"

"Looked good, all considered. I got off easier than your grandfather."

"He'll need to stay a few more days, for antibiotics. Grandpa thinks the leg is fine but he doesn't want to rile his surgeon, just in case more needs to be done."

"I'll look in on him tonight." Grant rolled the stir strip around his finger.

"Thanks, he'd like that. He was impressed with you, and I don't just mean as a physician. You bailed us out when you really didn't have to."

"A regular knight in shining armor." The stir strip sprang open, shooting drops of coffee across the small table.

Crystal smiled. Perhaps the modern-day equivalent. "Will Scott be long, you think?"

"No."

"Did he tell you where they were going to relocate me?" Crystal asked as she held the coffee near her nose and inhaled the strong aroma.

"No," Grant answered as he blotted the coffee drops with a napkin.

"What's going on?"

He shifted in his chair and looked at the television hanging on the wall, pulling at his lower lip.

"Grant?"

"Look," he began. "This isn't my idea. But the Sheriff wants to keep an eye on both of us."

"And?" There was more to the story, more that neither Grant Sands nor Scott Lang wanted to talk with her about. Grant was obviously uncomfortable, kind of cute—the rugged unshaven, macho, war veteran fidgeting around in his chair in front of her. "What?"

He jolted upright. "Well, they can't afford hotel rooms for both of us and the Sheriff wanted us in the same locality so they can cover us with one deputy at a time."

She crooked her head slightly and waited.

"So the suggestion was made that you stay at my townhouse." He added quickly. "I have three bedrooms and three bathrooms."

Crystal breathed slowly and tapped her upper front teeth while studying Grant. She had just been run out of her house by armed men. Shot at for the second time in as many days. And above all, she needed a shower and a bed.

"Fine," she said. "Can we leave now?"

Chapter 21

Panama City Country Club Estates

The sun beat down as noon approached. Crystal followed the Jeep and a Sheriff's department vehicle through a residential area replete with majestic oak trees heavily draped in Spanish moss. They turned into the Country Club gate. A uniformed guard waved them through. As she pulled into Grant's townhouse, he motioned for her to park her grandfather's truck in the right bay of the garage. Good idea.

The door closed behind her and she climbed from the truck, admiring the silver corvette convertible that sat in the left bay. Late summer heat had the interior of the garage baking like an oven. The door to the house opened with a relieving gush of cool air.

"No point advertising that you're here," Grant said.

Crystal climbed the few steps into the townhouse. The back was a bank of windows facing the expansive bay. White caps danced off the end of a weathered dock where a pelican sat lazily observing the water. Manicured grass and rich green holly bushes framed the picturesque view. The living room and sitting-area decorations tended toward leather and earth tones. Dean Quigley paintings of early Florida Indians hung at intervals, interrupted by displays of arrowheads and weaponry.

"I hope this doesn't offend you." He nervously picked up a stray cup and an anthropology magazine.

Crystal had seen these displays before in other homes and businesses. She walked slowly across the room. "I have nothing against collectors," she said, watching him over her left shoulder. "Most are done tastefully ... but occasionally you run into the shyster brokers

... basically grave robbers."

Grant cleared his throat.

"Your collection celebrates the life and struggles of the Indian," she said before he could speak. "I see no burial pots or sacred artifacts. You've attempted to honor those you study, not profit from them."

Grant stared awkwardly at her. What he was thinking she had no idea, she just felt sadness, and something else.

"Is that cinnamon I smell?" She twisted her head toward him.

"Yes, I suppose, cinnamon-flavored apple cider, I had one before work the other night." He held the empty cup up for her inspection. "Like some?"

"Only if you are."

Grant turned stiffly and opened the refrigerator, favoring his right side. Light from the kitchen window accentuated his cut profile as he poured cider from a large glass bottle. His forearm muscles stood out in chiseled relief. Tight glutes and athletic legs brought her back to the previous night when she'd glimpsed the smooth skin of his buttock while applying his dressing.

"I get the cider from Georgia," Grant said. "It's fresh and no preservatives, but definitely not low calorie." He smirked. "Not that you have to worry about calories." He moved about the compact kitchen easily, domestic in some respects, not a bad thing.

Crystal stroked her hand along a display case of largely intact pottery. Images of content ancients, women and children along the banks of St. Andrews Bay, leaped into her mind. In the correct time and setting she could be with them experiencing the peacefulness of the moment. He was watching her. She turned away from the display just as a whiff of smoldering pine logs teased her nostrils.

"Those were found by an old-time Cove resident when his house plot was excavated in the early 1920s," Grant said.

"They hold many wonderful memories."

Grant twisted his head briefly toward her, and then repeated the act.

Crystal smiled. "There are things about my heritage I don't understand," she tried to explain. "My grandpa says it will come in time. But it's still going to take some work before I'm completely able to accept the visions and insights." It was not much of an explanation. She walked to the granite kitchen counter and sat across from Grant.

"You never answered my question from the other day," he said. "Will you take over your grandfather's position with the tribe?"

Crystal did not answer. She couldn't. She didn't know. She stared at Grant for what seemed an eternity.

•

Grant reached for a package of cinnamon sticks as the pot of apple cider came to a boil. She was tired and he was not being a good host, pinning her down on touchy issues. "Well, let me get you this hot cider, and then I'll show you to your room ... the guest room," he corrected himself, unsure what connotation referring to the room as hers might have.

He'd never brought a woman back to his house. Hadn't thought of how the décor and furnishings would appear to a woman. He'd never considered himself in the dating market, yet alone evaluated his bachelor pad for its "chick" appeal.

Crystal nodded a weary head and settled her elbows on the counter, her chin resting on delicate interlaced fingers. Her eyes closed as she sighed. She seemed at peace, content even. "Does the guest bedroom have a bathtub?" she asked without opening her eyes.

"No, but my room does, a Jacuzzi tub."

"Watch it, buster." Her eyes opened wide.

Grant scrutinized her. She returned a spirited gaze, looking for a rise out of him. "I can't use the tub for a few days anyway." He pointed to his right hip. "My housekeeper was just in. Clean sheets and probably even a pile of clean towels. It's all yours. Just let me get a few things from the cabinet and my closet."

"You're a gentleman and a scholar, Doctor Grant Sands."

"Don't test me too much. Deep down I'm just a depressed, desperate, and deprived GI."

"Deprived of what and desperate for what?" She used a spunky tone and thankfully ignored the depression comment.

"Not of tender loving care. I had plenty of that last night, right down to the lingerie."

Crystal grabbed a hand towel and threw it at Grant. He caught it deftly without taking his gaze off her. She liked to tease, and if given a fight, she'd fight back.

He tuned to the stove, poured two cups of hot cider, and placed a fresh cinnamon stick in each. As he turned to Crystal the scent of sweet lilac, Crystal Blackrock, assaulted his senses like an aphrodisiac. His expression must have given him away.

•

The blue-grey was back in Grant's eyes, accentuated with a mischievous glint. She had started this tryst. *Cut it off quickly. Don't be a tease.* But she was enjoying the sexual banter with a virile, engaging hunk of a man, both of them probably visualizing a naked rendezvous in the Jacuzzi. Not going to happen. "I need about a half hour. You're working tonight, right?"

"Yeah, I'll hit the shower and crash in the guest room. Just make yourself at home in the master suite."

Crystal sensed a rise in Grant's heart rate. There was more. His eyes diverted, he thought he'd hidden the momentary window into his emotions and fears. He hadn't. But what Crystal perceived was impossible to interpret. His heart ached. His mind fought for control, though on the surface he appeared calm.

"I appreciate you opening your home to me like this. The Sheriff really put you on the spot there, didn't he?"

"I'm happy to help, any way I can." Blue-grey eyes studied her.

Outwardly nothing changed but the tension eased. It was uncanny and alarming that she should have such a connection with this man. Certainly they'd been through a lot together, and he was a man of medicine, which spoke of compassion and empathy.

But something here was tied to her struggle for harmony and the Sacred Way. What she didn't know and could not comprehend was how it all fit together, or even if it did. Perhaps it was just an assemblage of disconnected beliefs and sensitivities that had no association. Though she wanted to believe that she possessed the insight to see these relationships, she sorely wondered if she was gifted enough to find the common thread that held it all together.

The self-doubt was not new. She'd felt it throughout her adolescence and adulthood. It hadn't been there at age eleven when her grandmother first initiated her. Back then she had the confidence of youth. She knew she would be every bit the medicine person her grandmother and grandfather had been. Somewhere the journey had gotten derailed, but where? How?

Shaking her head, she rose. Sipping the warm cider, she inhaled deeply through her nose and tasted the sweet apple, the enticing cinnamon. "I'm a basket case. Promise me you won't take anything I say in this sleep-deprived state seriously. Or hold it against me tomorrow."

He smiled and raised his cider. "To making memories. May the next set be a little more tame, but yet still special."

"Why Doctor Sands, are you trying to be chivalrous?"

"Romantic, I thought, in a sort of lame way."

The blunt admission took Crystal by surprise. "Well … has the poor defenseless damsel stumbled into the lair of the evil giant?"

"Something like that, I guess." Grant rubbed the back of his neck and studied Crystal, one tired eyebrow drooping slightly. "Ditto on the sleep-deprived ramblings." He raised his glass in salute and limped toward a door off the great room. "The master suite is through the double doors."

He pointed to the left.

Chapter 22

Sand's Townhouse

Grant slept five hours and was awakened by gentle chimes from the clock radio. He limped slightly crossing the room, the skin and muscles of his hip pulling. He carefully covered the suture line against the pounding water of the shower, his regimen for the next few days. By the time he'd finished the pain had eased.

Shadows bathed the lawn as he closed the curtains on the windows to the bay. His thoughts wandered to Crystal. The soft contentment he had seen when she'd examined his collection of artifacts earlier reminded him once again of his grandmother. She likewise had always spoken with calm reverence around the sacred artifacts of her ancestors, cherished pieces that were capable of giving one a glimpse of those struggling natives who defined a true balance with nature and man.

A light emanated from the master suite, but no noise. He crept close and peeked in through the partially opened door. Crystal lay asleep on his bed, silky dark hair everywhere staking claim to his pillow. A sight, no matter how appealing, he was not prepared for —a woman in his bed. A prospect he had not entertained for years, since Jennifer Winthrop had left during his critical-care fellowship.

He'd carried a lot of baggage home from the war and the long hours in the hospital had not lent themselves to introspection and relationship building. On the surface Jennifer had tried to understand, tried to give him time. But in the end she was not up to the task. Would any woman be?

Grant turned on the bathroom light. A safety light at night made it easier for him to re-orient himself in strange surroundings.

Better than the blinding flash that had awakened him in combat. She looked more peaceful in his bed than he ever did. She wore one of his old triathlon shirts—large. It revealed her upper bosom rising and falling deliberately. He turned the ceiling fan to low and the main lights off. The glow from the bathroom accentuated Crystal's smooth skin and painted thin shadows of eyelashes across her cheeks. Beautiful. Delicate and fragile, as was all life.

Before he knew what he was doing he leaned and gently kissed her forehead. He was immediately inundated with the fragrances of sweet honey and crisp burning pine.

Quickly, he stood up, bolts of multicolored light bursting behind his eyes! He blinked and all that remained was a sugary tingle on the tip of his tongue. She didn't move. What was that, some mystical connection? And what was he doing?

He was lucky she didn't sit up and smack him in the face. Softly he backed away, pulled away. Urges deep inside implored him to take her in his arms and re-experience the moment. Something unearthly was drawing him to this conflicted and temperamental woman, a magnetism of fearsome power.

Chapter 23

Community Medical Center, Panama City

Amir didn't like it here in America, just like he hadn't liked his years in England. There was no hate in his heart for the English-speaking infidels. If they would just stay on their side of the world and keep their ideals of godliness to themselves, life would be much better for everyone, and for Islam—or at least for most of the Islamic world. Unfortunately, there were always fringe fanatics, like the ones at his mosque, the ones who had assigned him the blessed task.

Getting to America had been easy but dirty, a rusty freighter out of Santa Domingo two weeks earlier followed by three hours in the pitching bait-well of a fishing trawler. Lying hidden in the dark, cramped compartment had felt like being in a coffin not to mention the retching and vomiting. He'd prayed to Allah for fresh air. What had the people's movement gotten him into?

Finally the powerful engines had throttled back. Blood rushed to his head as the boat decelerated in its own wake. Commands in Spanish were followed by the scurrying of feet on the deck and a bump on what the Captain of the boat had called the port side. They had arrived in America.

The whining of an electric drill signaled his release. A short sweating Hispanic crewman put the sleeve of a dirty fatigue jacket over his mouth and nose as he'd removed the floor panel above Amir, waving his hand to dissipate the stench.

Standing strained Amir's muscles. Leg spasms abated when he'd forced them straight. A three-quarter moon cast an eerie pall across a riverbank. Tall shadowed pines waved beneath a panorama of stars. Indistinct figures move between the trees, several crouched unmoving. Hungrily he'd sucked in the cool air, straightening his shoulders.

His rescuer pointed with the drill toward a dilapidated dock to which the boat was tied. On unstable legs he'd crawled over the railings. Splinters attacked his knees as he scurried onto the wobbling platform. Operations were underway on the detritus-covered shore amongst vegetation he had only seen in books and flower shops.

The pot-bellied, scraggly captain kicked at a dead body lying half in the river, and barked a few orders to a wide-eyed, younger man gripping an assault rifle. His fatigue-jacket rescuer clamored out of the boat with an armful of chains and headed to a dark recess where two or three figures huddled, trembling. This was an unholy place.

The captain pulled a red plastic container from his pocket and snapped it open. Inside were a half-dozen syringes. He glanced up and gestured his head toward a truck barely visible up the slope of the forest. Clearly, it was time to continue his journey.

Three days later, Amir now stood in the shadow of the parking-lot fence. Halogen lights cut the night. He wiped sweaty hands on his pant legs. An idling tractor trailer of cabbage and lettuce sat a half mile to the north behind a discount supermarket. The Mexican truck driver had been well paid. He could wait another hour. There was something that must be done. Moist air off the Gulf blew his hair as he studied the multiple wings and connecting corridors of the American hospital. Pine needles crackled under his feet as he shifted nervously.

It would be easy. He'd done it thousands of times. Every hospital was basically the same. Medical and surgical floors, an emergency room, operating rooms, and the critical care area, the latter usually centrally located for quick access. X-ray machines and special intensive care equipment needed to be readily available, delays could not be tolerated. Personnel came and left the areas throughout the day and night. Shift change was busy as were visiting hours, but the night shift operated on autopilot, unless an emergency developed.

Then all Hell broke loose, generally. He'd know within minutes if that was the case though.

He wiped his hands once again on the rough fabric of his pants, picked the Community Health Center bag out of the back of a silver pickup, and adjusted the strap over his shoulder. It was the little things that counted. He strutted with intent toward the door next to the loading dock.

Chapter 24

Sand's Townhouse

Crystal awoke with a start. Darkness encompassed her except for a slight glow from the foot of the bed. Grant's bed. She sat and listened. Nothing. The blackness of the night was cut only by light from the master bathroom. She inhaled the balmy maleness of the bed-spread and room, her senses on high alert.

His presence lingered.

He had touched her but was gone now—had been for hours. She sat up and pulled the sheets close, comforted by his scent but still lonely. It was hard to put a finger on her emotions. Certainly she had not enjoyed playing cat-and-mouse with human traffickers. But on some level she'd been comforted, felt secure with Grant at her side.

"He can sure get under your skin," she said aloud.

The clock radio beside the bed read one o'clock. Nearly twelve hours since she had succumbed to the exhaustion of the previous day. She wouldn't be able to fall asleep again, so best get up for awhile.

She picked her way about the bedroom of typical male furnishings. A solid cherry dresser topped by an antler-horn lamp, a framed graphic depicting the evolution of arrowheads, kind of sparse. She headed to the kitchen for tea or maybe more apple cider.

Grant's presence hung heavily throughout the townhouse. But there was more, a lingering gloom, a somber melancholy that chilled her soul. Not Grant Sands but some essence of the dead, *este-elvte*. Grant was haunted by souls deeply out of harmony. She did not perceive them in the house with her but their past presence was unmistakable.

A note sat on the counter.

"Make yourself at home. There's salad in the refrigerator and some canned foods in the pantry. If you are up and about give me a call on my cell and let me know how you're faring. My hip seems to be okay, after a few ibuprofens. I'm sure it would be even better if you'd been awake to work your magic."

The last comment was followed by a hand written smiley face. Did he mean for her to call him, in the middle of the night? But he was working the night shift and would be up. She dialed the number he'd left on the bottom of the note.

•

What had possessed him to kiss Crystal Blackrock while she slept? Thank God she hadn't awakened. What would he have done? How could he have convinced her that he was not some pervert attacking a woman in her sleep? A woman he was supposed to be protecting—a woman reaching perilously deep into his unsettled soul. Man! He'd been roped into that one very smoothly by the Sheriff. He'd think twice next time about jumping so quickly. Well, at least she didn't know what he'd done. Honey and burnt pine continued to linger in his senses.

Rounds went well and he sipped coffee as he scrolled through digitized X-rays on the intensive care unit. He leaned back in the wheeled reclining chair and surveyed the staff, his thoughts wandering in a confusing pattern. His war-zone sensitivity had been tweaked through the evening by one particular individual he didn't recognize. The man wore hospital scrubs but his badge was flipped backward and Grant wasn't sure if he was a nurse, technician, or just an orderly. There had been some staff turnover on the units and a number of the nurses were travelers, typically from up north trying to get out ahead of the cold weather.

The dark-skinned man was watching him. But when Grant had turned toward him, he was either gone or walking away.

Frustrated, he eased back from the computer screen and swallowed a mouthful of coffee. The reading alcove was dark, allowing close scrutiny of the X-rays. He almost didn't see the man standing in the shadows.

"Doctor Sands?" the man asked in a clipped tone, a Far Eastern accent.

"Yes … " Grant extended his hand.

The man hesitated and then took the hand and shook it apprehensively. He did not offer his name. Instead he shifted his gaze over Grant's shoulder, checking to see if they were being observed.

"Can I help you with something?" Grant asked.

"Perhaps," the man said looking back over his shoulder.

"Do you work here?" Grant asked. "Are you assigned on the unit?"

The Arab-appearing man eased the tension in his shoulders. "I am Doctor Abdul Patel," he said and nervously smiled. He eased back into the shadow of the alcove.

"What brings you to the unit so late, Abdul? Can I call you Abdul?"

"Certainly," Cold dark eyes did not blink. His tongue moistened his lip.

Grant wished he had his .45. He'd been scrutinized like this before, in Kandahar and Kabul.

"I have come to talk with you, Doctor Sands."

"About a patient?" Grant asked.

Once again the shifting gaze swept the unit and returned to Grant. "About Mr. Blackrock and his daughter."

"Granddaughter," Grant said.

The man smiled again, this time less nervous, more sincere. "And a lovely granddaughter she is."

Grant thought to explain that he was not involved medically in Mr. Blackrock's care, but somehow didn't think that was going to make any difference to Doctor Patel. There was more to this than a medical consultation. Throw the man a bone. "They are involved in a criminal investigation."

"Yes, crimes against humanity. No matter what your religion, God does not allow the slaughter or defiling of his children, even if they are infidels." His hands remained in sight. He rubbed stubbled whiskers. "First, an attempt must be made to convert them to the ways of Mohammad. And killing and plundering should not be a money-making venture."

"Are you really a doctor?" Grant asked, certain this was all headed in the wrong direction.

"Yes, a surgeon from Waziristan, the northern mountains of

Pakistan." The smile was back. "And you, Doctor ... combat experience?"

Where was this going? Who was this late-night interrogator? "Afghanistan," Grant played along.

"Oh, Pat Tillman, the mountains, and Special Forces?"

"Not exactly."

"The Afghan mountains or the Pakistani mountains?"

"The Hind Kush, for the record."

The man nodded. "I have a good practice in Pakistan. But I have been asked to do a special project for my people." His facial muscles slackened. He cast his eyes down and when he looked up they held a hollow darkness that was emphasized by the slump of his shoulders and a fatalistic sigh.

Grant waited.

"The safety of my family depends on me completing my project." Remorse filled his tone.

"What are you trying to tell me, Abdul?"

"They would have sold her into slavery and taken your organs if they'd been able to capture you. The old man they'd have just killed, like the man in the river."

"You're talking about the traffickers from the other night?" Grant sat straight up in his chair. "How do you know about this?"

"I've been sent to complete a project, which has nothing to do with trafficking in slavery and body organs."

"What are you talking about?" Grant asked, the muscles of his neck and back tightening.

"Women and organ donors are trafficked out through the Gulf of Mexico. People like me, for a price, are smuggled in. I had no idea what the men who brought me up that river had planned for their trip out." Doctor Patel, if that was his name, rubbed his hands firmly and blew a prayer into his intertwined fingers. He made gnawing motions with his mouth, successfully holding back raw emotions that obviously wanted to flood out.

"You should go to the police." Grant realized how idiotic the statement was as soon as he'd said it. So did Dr. Patel.

Tension eased from Dr. Patel's neck. His voice became stronger. "One of the men mentioned the Blackrocks. And, I heard them speak of shifting their operation to the Louisiana coast, near New Orleans. It's up to you now, Dr. Sands."

Grant looked the man in the eyes. Fire stared back. No doubt the man was who he said he was, except for the name.

Grant's cell phone rang. He looked down at the calling number, his home phone, Crystal. When he looked back up Dr. Abdul Patel was gone. The muscles of Grant's neck ached and his stomach felt hollow.

Chapter 25

Sands' Townhouse

"Hello. Your note said to call. I hope I didn't wake you," Crystal said.

"No, just looking at some X-rays. Did you sleep okay?"

His voice sounded clipped as if he were preoccupied, not a good time for a deep discussion. "Long and hard, apparently." The microwave beeped and she removed a cup of brewing tea. "They said my grandfather might be released sometime today."

"Would the two of you head back out to the farm?"

"I don't know. I probably need to talk to the Sheriff about that. What do you think?"

He didn't answer immediately. Was he trying to decide if he should go back out to the farm with them? Or was he debating what the Sheriff would expect them to do?

"I mean, would the Sheriff want us at the farm this quickly after what happened?" she asked.

"I think he'll still want to watch you. I don't know where that's gonna work out best."

He was holding something back—a strain in his voice—deliberate, calculating. She wasn't playing this game with him. "What's going on, Grant?"

"Boy, you're something else, aren't you? Don't give a guy an inch."

"Yeah, that's what my cousins always told me." Crystal revealed a criticism that had also been leveled at her by the rare boyfriend she'd had.

Grant chuckled. "Right … well, there's been a development here at the hospital that I think I'll need to talk with the Sheriff about."

"Is my grandfather okay? Has something happened?"

"No, nothing has happened. I'm sorry. I didn't mean to scare you. He's just fine." He told Crystal about the visit from Dr. Abdul Patel.

"So, he was with the smugglers ... at some point anyway." Crystal said. She was completely awake now.

"Looks that way."

"And they know it was my grandpa and me at the river." She swallowed hard. "The one he talked about, that recognized us, must be their local contact."

"Could be he also owns a tan or beige SUV or truck." Grant paused on the phone. "There can't be that many of those in the area. I occasionally see a tan extended cab truck in the doctor's parking lot ... but I don't remember any SUVs that color."

Crystal cleared her throat. "Do you think this Doctor Patel is some sort of Muslim terrorists? Why else would he be with people like that? Surely he's not part of their organization."

"I think he's been recruited because he speaks English and understands how things work in America. He probably did some of his medical training in the United States or Britain."

"He took a big risk coming to the hospital to talk with you," she said.

"Odd, you know. I've heard of honor among thieves, but among terrorists?"

"He put his whole family at risk to tell you about the smugglers and give you information that might be valuable to the police. Unless there is something else going on none of us are aware of."

Silence. What a dangerous world the terrorist came from, a world where people had no choice but to obey fanatical demands. And yet in the secretive labyrinth that was terrorist insurgency, a spark of humanity and true godliness existed. Good men came from every walk of life, or so it would seem.

"Well, we need to make sure his effort is not in vain," Grant said. "It's men like him that hold the real hope for our world, men who see the truth for what it really is, and not a bastardized interpretation by some fanatic with an agenda."

"Should I meet you at the hospital in the morning?"

"I'm calling the Sheriff now, though I doubt if they'll find any trace of the good doctor."

"Do you think he's right? I mean about the smugglers heading toward New Orleans?"

"I hope so."

After hanging up, Crystal stared for a long time at her reflection in the windows. The spicy fragrance of herbal tea teased her nostrils. What brought about the evil and brutality that led men to kill and sell women into slavery? She'd had none of that in her upbringing. Sure, the occasional murder or rape, usually spurred on by some family argument or an alcohol-induced rage. She'd never experienced it in her family, but had seen it in the community —on the reservation.

What did Grant experience in Afghanistan? Had he witnessed wholesale death, rape, and pillaging? What did that do to one's perception of mankind?

She wandered through the house touching chairs and books, artifact guides, Tony Hillerman novels. The essence of Grant Sands was far away in these items. He was living in this house but the true spirit that was the *este-fv'tcvn*, the man, was not here. For a man to unify his life he had to be in harmony, not only with the surroundings, but with himself.

Grant was in turmoil, not comfortable anywhere right now. What baggage had he brought from the war? Could any of that be wiped clean? Or was he, like many veterans, destined to ramble through life a ghost of his former self, a shell of what he could be? Stunned by the ravages of war into a mere wandering beast, looking for a warm dry spot to rest his weary body, only to pull his hollow soul up the next morning to face a day that held no hope.

In the laundry room she picked up his soiled shirt from the night before. It smelled of the musky forest and of manhood. She held the fabric to her nose and inhaled. What she didn't detect was fear or the hopelessness she dreaded might be there. She did discern anger and loneliness, almost an adolescent sentiment of disillusion. Truly this was a man adrift. For all the outward appearances of calm detachment, of obvious intelligence, Grant was a ship without a port.

Her heart ached for his private suffering. Akin to how she felt after her mother's death. But she had been rescued from that abyss by the love and guidance of her grandmother and grandfather. Was that what Grant needed, love and support, a good woman? Crystal ran her hand through her hair and sipped the tea, the warm liquid easing the tension in her throat. Was she a good woman, capable of leading this man back from the brink? She had been at one time. Where had she lost her way? Where was her path? Her grandfather had repeatedly told her the time would come. *Be patient. Keep your mind open to the possibilities.*

She stood at the windows looking out to the bay. There was a connection here. In the home of this damaged war veteran. She strained through a dull roaring in her head to glimpse a strange and ill-defined insight that struggled to reveal itself. Drawn to the water, she threw open the door and a cooling breeze off the darkened bay enveloped her.

Soft grass caressed her feet as she gazed up to a cloudless sky. Over the blackness of the bay the stars glowed brilliantly. The constellations captured her as they had when she was a young girl on the Blackrock farm. Suddenly, with conviction, she went to the garage and retrieved a rolled blanket from behind the seat of her grandfather's truck.

Next to the inky blackness of the bay waters she spread the woven and decorated blanket on the ground. Carefully she placed several items from the roll on the grass and faced the assemblage to the east. Peacefulness descended on her as she arranged her medicine poles at the four corners, cane reeds topped with feathers. The poles were old, dating from her youth. Memories of happier times inundated her.

She had spent numerous hours, days, preparing them under her grandmother's direction. It was time to call upon them once again to help her. A fifth pole was laid on the blanket next to an eagle feather and two small gourds.

Finally Crystal sat facing the east and removed measured portions of cedar slices and sage from the gourds. The familiar aromas pleasantly tickled her senses. She started a small fire in a pottery bowl. The flame danced lazily, and bittersweet emanations soaked into her hair and clothing.

Tobacco sprinkled over the embers produced a pungent smoke. She directed it ever so delicately with the gentle massage of an eagle feather. There she sat through the early morning hours awaiting the rising sun, opening her mind and soul, preparing herself to give heartfelt thanks for the wonderful gifts of a new sunrise and another day to bask in the glory of nature.

Ironically, she sat in Grant Sands' backyard and implored the Creator and the universe to reveal to her the answers she so much desired. She and her grandfather would need a cleansing ceremony.

The negative and brutalized *puyvfekcv* of the dead man at the river tainted their souls. As did that of the man she had killed the previous night. As soon as her grandfather was able they would contact Micah Kanache, fast for several days, and build a sweat house next to a pure running stream. It would take days to sweat the sickness from their bodies. And, all sweat must be washed away by running water before it dried.

This, her grandmother had taught her.

Chapter 26

Community Medical Center

Sheriff Tumley crumpled the paper cup and threw it with vengeance at the trash can. It had taken twenty minutes for the dispatcher to awaken him with Grant's message. Sitting now in the medical conference room, at the opposite end of the table from Grant, he received the news he expected. No signs of the mysterious Doctor Patel.

Discarded scrubs were found in receptacles throughout the hospital, any of them could be Dr. Patel's. As for the hospital badge, every staff lounge and locker room had two or three white coats or smocks with name tags affixed. Which one Dr. Patel had used was anyone's guess. The crime-scene crew had found a myriad of finger prints where Grant had observed the terrorist, several appeared clear, but probably none belonged to the Pakistani doctor.

Grant watched the clock tick past seven, his shift was up. "Look Sheriff, I was sitting down. I don't even know if he was five foot tall or closer to six. I think he had several days' growth of facial hair. But of course that could be gone by now." He shrugged. "Sorry."

Holding the handle of his gun like a cane, Tumley paced about the small room. "The DMV says they've got 632 trucks and SUVs in the panhandle registered as tan or beige. And, that's assuming the vehicle is registered locally."

"It is someone who knows the Blackrocks by sight," Grant said. "At least the local contact must."

"So I guess the next question is how important to them is this local contact." The Sheriff stopped his pacing. "If he's not important he may just end up as another body. End of that story ... we should be so lucky."

Tumley sat on the edge of the table and glared at Grant. "So, you think some terrorist organization paid the traffickers to smuggle this Patel guy into the States?"

"That's what it seems like."

The Sheriff stood, shook his nearly shaven head, and rolled his bloodshot eyes with an air of surrender. "Deputy Cross called in about twenty minutes ago. Miss Blackrock is headed to the hospital, should be here any minute."

"Any news from their farm?"

"I'll go over that with y'all once she's here. Can you remember anything else about this Arab doctor that might open up another lead?"

"As I said, he was smuggled in for some apparent terrorist purpose. He just couldn't stomach what the smugglers were up to. He didn't mention anything more specific than being a surgeon from Waziristan."

"Well, Homeland Security has been notified and they'll be here soon to interview you … probably with the FBI."

"I've been there before," Grant answered.

The Sheriff cracked his neck left and right and then nodded.

Grant's cell phone chimed and he pushed the text message retrieve button. "That's the surgical floor. Miss Blackrock is in her grandfather's room and asking for me."

"Go ahead, I'll be over in a few minutes," Tumley said.

On the way to Will Blackrock's room Grant called his partner, Chuck Byron, and gave him the quick lowdown on their patient census. He begged off rounds, but said he'd be on his cell phone.

Crystal was tidying up her grandfather's room. She looked radiant—blue jeans, a burgundy camisole top, and matching jean jacket. His gaze lingered on her too long. Both she and her grandfather noticed. He smiled. She blushed.

"Did Crystal tell you about the local connection?" Grant asked. "Apparently they're worried about you identifying them."

Will nodded. It was clear the topic had been discussed, probably heatedly.

"When are they going to finally spring you out of here?" Grant asked.

"None to soon, tomorrow morning, I hope," Will answered.

"Another day of antibiotics, they say."

"Oh." Grant turned to Crystal, who shrugged. "Are you staying here all day?" The question to Crystal came out before he realized how it probably sounded. "I mean … I'm off today … actually for the next six days. My shift rotation is up." Man, he was babbling. "If you need anything I'd be happy to see what I can do." With that he exhaled and looked from Crystal to her grandfather.

"Don't hang around here for me," her grandfather said, eyeing Crystal. "No point in both of us getting cabin fever. I'm gonna try and reach Micah. We need to set up a cleansing."

Crystal crossed to where Grant stood at the foot of the bed. She wrapped her hands around his arm. He fought the shiver that ran up his spine. "Doctor Sands was the perfect host last night, Grandpa." She beamed up at Grant who towered over her. "I can't impose on him anymore. Otherwise I'll have to start paying rent."

They laughed.

Crystal stayed next to him and stole a glance. Something was different with her today. Of course, every other day he'd been with her they had been dealing with murderous smugglers. Maybe this was the true Crystal Blackrock—sensitive, confident, and charming. That might be more than Grant was ready for, but first he had to get over the war and Jennifer Winthrop. It was not a lifestyle he wished to live indefinitely. Was there a light at the end of the murky tunnel that had been his life these past five years? A lump formed in his throat, forcing him to swallow.

He glanced at Crystal, dark pools in her eyes tugged him deeply. The lump refused to go down.

•

Crystal was trying to put together Grant's reaction to her casual touch when Sheriff Tumley knocked on the hospital door and raised bushy salt-and-pepper eyebrows. "Okay to come in, folks?" She was taken aback, as was her grandfather.

Grant threw his hands up. "Sorry, I forgot to tell you the Sheriff wanted to follow up on some things this morning. Are you up to it, Mr. Blackrock?"

"Shoot," Will Blackrock said, then wrinkled his face. "Probably a bad choice of words."

The Sheriff chuckled as Grant and Crystal nodded.

She let go of Grant and sat next to her grandfather, patted his arm, and smiled warmly at Grant. "What do you have, Sheriff? Good news, I hope."

"Mind if we sit?" he asked.

Grant retrieved a second chair from the nurses' station. Crystal remained seated on the bed next to her grandfather.

"The body on your farm was a middle-aged Hispanic male, no identification, but some tattoos that could lead somewhere." He didn't seem very convincing.

Grant listened intently. Crystal could visualize him at a tactical briefing, taking notes, checking facts.

"And now we have this new wrinkle of the benevolent terrorist." Sheriff Tumley paced back and forth, slammed his hat on the empty chair. "If I didn't know better, I'd think someone was playing me."

Her grandfather looked at Crystal with a furrowed brow.

"My grandfather and I have racked our brains and cannot think of anyone we know who could be involved in something like this. Of course we have many Hispanics and Muslims in the area. And just about everyone we know has a truck, SUV, or four-wheel drive."

Grant stood and walked to the window. "For all we know the local guy could be Caucasian. Patel never volunteered if he was a smuggler or fellow terrorist."

"The good Doctor Patel is nowhere to be found this mornin'," the Sheriff said. "We've notified Homeland Security and the FBI. Doctor Sands will need to meet with them sometime today."

"Any idea when?" Grant asked.

"I haven't even heard back from them yet. But I do know they're active from the message traffic we're receiving."

Crystal placed a hand on her grandfather's good leg. "Any news on the smugglers heading west toward Louisiana?"

"This is confidential, really all of this is, if you know what I mean," Tumley began. "We've got a make on the tires and wheel base that suggests at least one of the vehicles used by the traffickers was a heavily loaded, late model, extended cab Chevy 1500. That doesn't match any of the vehicles we've found in the river so far ... There is an APB out for the Southeast. But that is a pretty common truck around here."

He stood and flipped through some pages of printouts, tapping his teeth.

Crystal stood and walked behind Grant. He sat rigid in the chair, almost at attention. She placed her hand on a shoulder that felt hard as stone. She massaged her thumbs into the resisting muscles as they watched the Sheriff re-consult his paperwork. She was making little headway on the tight muscles. Grant rotated his head as she massaged. If they'd been alone, she imagined he would have purred.

"Can my grandfather and I go back to the farm when he's discharged? Do you think it would be safe?" she asked.

"We've had no confirmation that the smugglers have left the area. For now we have to assume they are still here. And of course the local accomplice is still unidentified and at large." One of Tumley's scruffy eyebrows raised. "Can we impose on you for another day, Doctor?"

The muscles in Grant's shoulders began to soften. Amazing. In a situation that should have caused even more tension and stress, Grant was relaxing. The prospect of spending more time with Crystal actually was having a calming effect on this rugged modern-day warrior. She redoubled her massage efforts.

"Are you continuing the police surveillance?" Grant asked.

"Of course, and having the two of you at the townhouse makes that a lot easier," the Sheriff said.

Grant rotated back and forth in the office chair, pulling on his lower lip. "If the terrorist knew I was involved, we have to assume the smugglers would also know."

"Right, we've looked at other options, hotels and such, but we still feel your townhouse is the most defensible," Tumley said.

"Oh yeah, I agree." Grant nodded.

The Sheriff and Grant continued to make their plans.

Crystal slid back onto the bed with her grandfather. She'd have to let the clinic know she couldn't get back. Stacks of insurance denials and records requests would cover her desk. It could wait. They'd call if something important came up. "Is this all right for you, Grandpa?"

"I want whatever is safest for you," he said and then smiled like the Cheshire Cat. Leaning close he whispered, "It'll give you a little more time with the doctor."

Crystal socked him lightly on the shoulder. "Grandpa, stop!

You're no matchmaker."

"Granddaughter, keep your mind and heart open to the possibilities." He patted her hand gently.

The Sheriff and Grant had finished their plans.

Grant took a step toward Crystal and her grandfather. "I guess we'll need to head back to the townhouse when you've finished visiting … unless you want to stay here through the morning."

Her grandfather tossed the crumpled morning newspaper on the foot of the bed. "Oh bull, you go ahead, young lady. No point in both of us being bored out of our minds."

Crystal pointed at her grandfather with a stern scowl, ever the instigator. She hadn't had a chance to talk with him about the connection she felt to the bluff and bay near Grant's townhouse, as if she'd been there before. She'd experienced feelings like that when she was in contact with the ancients, but frequently could not discern if the perceptions were hers or those of her ancestors.

"Are you ready to leave right now?" Crystal asked.

"No, I should check in with my relief to see if he has any questions, maybe in twenty or thirty minutes."

She nodded.

When Grant and the Sheriff left, Crystal sat next to her grandfather. She took a deep breath to calm her nerves and organize her thoughts. "A strange thing happened last night, Grandpa."

"With the doctor?"

"No, he was here at the hospital working." Crystal pulled her chair closer to the bed. "I had an overwhelming calling last night in his backyard, standing under the stars and looking out into the dark bay."

He pursed his lips and squinted. "Perhaps it is starting. I have known medicine people who got the call late in life, some in their fifties."

"But at such a location?" Crystal shook her head. "And the draw was more intense than I have ever experienced. The spirits were so close, clearer than I've ever felt them."

"Did you prepare the sacred ground?"

"I did, as crazy as it sounds. Right there in the middle of the Country Club, in the doctor's backyard." She stood and paced, stopping in front of her grandfather. "As soon as I began the chanting to call the Creator to enlighten me the energy exploded. My heart raced and I tingled all over, even into my chest and stomach. I've never had that fantastic of a connection."

He was sitting up straight now on the bed, ignoring his injured leg. "And did you learn anything? Did the spirits show you the way?"

"Really, Grandpa, it was so intense I haven't completely taken it all in yet." Crystal sat next to him on the bed. "Grandma was there and many of the ancients. And I don't understand, but I sensed the presence of Grant's relatives as well. Could that be possible?"

Her grandfather cocked his head and stared blankly out the window. She honestly had never seen him unsure of himself. It was a little disconcerting.

"Where is this Country Club?" he asked.

"It's on North Bay. The townhouse sits up on a small bluff that looks out over the water."

"It looks north from the bluff?"

"Yes, across toward the timberland that borders the bay on that side."

"Could you see the sunrise this morning?"

"It was glorious. I could have stayed all day."

"Do you think if you were there this evening you could see the sun set?"

"Probably, the bluff is on a point of land and you can see out over the bay to the east and west."

He was on his feet now, struggling to look out the window that just happened to face north. "I've heard of such a place, never seen it. But there are stories from the ancients of a very sacred bluff that overlooks the bay. A bluff that allows a vantage of both the rising and setting sun. It was one of the most sacred of ceremonial sites before the settlement of the area."

"Could this be it? I've never heard this story before." Crystal's shoulders sank under the awesome prospect of such a discovery, for her personally and for the Creek people.

"It might just be. I'll make some calls. But I don't know if anyone still alive has any experience with this … It was really long ago that I heard of it."

"It's magical, Grandpa." Her cheeks strained with a glowing smile. "There must be something to it, has to be."

"I am happy for you, Granddaughter. It may be your time to find the Path. It won't be easy, but at least now perhaps it'll be more clear."

Chapter 27

Northern Panama City

Crystal followed Grant's Jeep through a preset course, first a residential area then a series of warehouses near the railroad. Deputy Cross again trailed them but left, at some apparently strategic location, only to fall back in behind before they entered the County Club. Cross backed into a tree-lined parking area near the fitness trail, just down from the doctor's townhouse. Crystal once again pulled the truck into the garage.

Grant was at the garage door into the house, holding it open. "Welcome back," he said, smiling.

Sunshine angled into the kitchen and family room as Crystal squeezed past. She couldn't suppress a feeling of trepidation. He had touched her while she slept, of that she was certain. But she didn't know to what extent. Did he just pull a cover over her shoulder or was it something more intimate?

Grant busied himself in the kitchen filling a pot with water and tossing away a soggy filter of old coffee grounds.

"How was your night?" she asked to break the ice.

"Quiet, actually. I never really get to sleep, though sometimes I catch a quick 'cat nap.'"

Crystal imagined a calm sleeping Grant, chest rising and falling rhythmically. She'd spent the night with men before, some appeared angelic as they slept. Others snored and flung their limbs about like lumberjacks. "So you sleep during the day then?"

"Mostly when I first get home—till about two or three in the afternoon."

"Well, don't let me crimp your schedule," Crystal said. "I'll be quiet as a butterfly."

"I'm off the rotation for the next week. So, I might snooze a few hours before meeting with the FBI and Homeland Security, but I'll catch up fine tonight."

"Are you sleeping now or later?"

"First I'm gonna hit the shower and get the grime of the medical center off, then maybe a few hours. I don't really know when they'll call." He placed a new filter with fresh grounds in the coffee maker and then headed to the guest bedroom.

Cleanliness was a must in a man. What was she thinking? Grant was going to be her man? She wouldn't even be in his home except for the murders. Sure he was tall, buff, and available. But definitely conflicted and an Ivy League-type guy to boot.

She took advantage of the time to wash and dry her hair. She removed her shirt and wrapped a towel from the master bath around her. Grant's wimpy hair dryer, thirteen hundred and seventy-five watts, was like torture. Finally she turned the noisy thing off, probably just before it self-destructed. The mugginess of the bathroom gave way to a glorious coolness as she threw open the door to the master suite, arching her back to the cool air. A cough sounded behind her. She spun around and confronted Grant—in a towel and nothing else.

She dropped her towel to the floor, gasped, and threw her hands across her breasts but not before presenting him a full-on view of her feminine attributes. "What are you doin'?" she sputtered, pulling the towel back over her.

"I knocked. You were in the bathroom with the hair dryer running. I just needed a clean change of clothes. Sorry."

The fullness in the front of his towel increased. Whatever!

"Well," she stammered. "It is your room." She smiled. Why had she said that?

"If you're okay then, I'll just grab a few things," Grant said.

Six-pack abdominals, ample pecs, and a sensual two day-growth of beard—she was staring, probably blushing also. Say something. He flashed a smile, straight white teeth and lips that had to be creamy and tender.

"Umm ... oh ... Yeah. I mean, hey. We're both adults." *Stupid, Crystal—stupid, stupid, stupid.* She turned and marched back into the bathroom, closing the door.

When she came back out, tank top on this time, Grant was back in the guest bedroom. A trace of men's shampoo and Irish Spring soap hung in the closet. Crystal lingered, savoring the images the smells concocted, pleasant and reassuring.

She entered the great room with apprehension. What would she say or stumble through this time? The guest room door was closed and no light shone from underneath, he must be trying to sleep.

On the counter in the kitchen, Crystal picked up an eighteen hundred and seventy-five watt hair dryer that had mysteriously materialized. What the heck! How did he know that?

On a rack, next to the back door, hung a fishing cap with side panels for the sun. With the hat and sunglasses from her purse, she figured she would not be recognized. The scattered white caps and lazy moving clouds out on the bay beckoned her. The grass again felt soft on her bare feet. She wandered down the low bluff toward the bay, picking her way carefully onto the dock, avoiding splinters and the occasional protruding nail. A light breeze off the bay fluttered the reeds at the water's edge.

It was serene and disarming. Her lungs filled with an airy freshness. She sat for more than an hour allowing nature—the sun, wind, earth, and water—to conduct her as they saw fit, truly a magical location.

"Hey, lady."

Crystal was bolted back to the present. She turned to see a man in a suit and tie standing at the base of the dock. "Yes, can I help you?"

"Yeah, you can help me and my wife," the stocky man said.

"I'm not sure I understand. I don't live here, just visiting."

"You're stayin' with the doc?" The man raised an eyebrow and screwed up his mouth.

Who was this man? What was he after? Certainly he didn't look like one of the smugglers or a terrorist.

"Look. I'm Frank. I live next door." He walked out on the dock and offered his hand.

Crystal rose and took the hand tentatively.

He shook hers vigorously. "I came to let the air conditioning guy in. I work at Wells Fargo Bank, in Lynn Haven."

It all seemed aboveboard. She'd never been in a protected situation before so wasn't sure what to expect. She looked toward the fitness trail where Deputy Cross was stationed. It was obscured by the side of the house. She was on her own. This was not a threat, she was certain of that. "What can I do for you, Frank?"

"That was you last night ... right?"

"You mean out back here?" Crystal began to see where this was headed.

"With the ceremony and all the chantin' and stuff." He waffled his hands like a magician.

"Yes, that was me."

"I'd seen the doc leave earlier. Figured he was at work, ya know." The man loosened his tie against the heat but left his suit jacket on. "With all the Indian stuff going on around here, I wasn't sure, you know, if somebody hadn't snuck past the guards and started some sort of sit-in or whatever they do."

"Indian stuff?" Crystal repeated.

"You probably don't know since you're just visiting and all. But you are Indian, right?"

"I'm a Creek."

"Yeah, well, you woke the wife and me last night. She's a light sleeper. I could hardly hear you, but Danielle couldn't get back to sleep." He rolled up his pretty-boy eyes and gestured his styled hair toward the townhouse that adjoined Grant's. "Anyway, maybe you could move around to the side of his place."

"You mean with any nighttime activities," Crystal said.

"Right, yeah, that would really help ... not that I really minded." The side of his mouth crept up into a smile and his eyebrow jumped again.

"Sure, Frank. Tell your wife she's safe. No Indian attacks or anything."

He pointed at Crystal and winked.

She worked to create an expression she hoped would pass for a smile.

Frank hurried up to his townhouse, stopped, and talked briefly with a technician bent over an air conditioning unit, turned, and waved at Crystal.

"Indian stuff." Where did these people come from? Indian culture existed in every state of the United States. If these people ever took the time to look.

Chapter 28

Sand's townhouse

Grant flipped the sizzling bacon for the third time. The sweet aroma of the cooking pork filled the small kitchen. A moist puff of Bay air rattled the blinds as the patio door opened quietly. He pushed up the sleeves of his casual shirt to his elbows and raised the spatula above his head. "What'll it be, eggs, omelet, or maybe French toast?"

"I thought you'd still be sleeping," Crystal said.

"Too nice of a day for that. Good disguise," he said, remembering his first impression of Crystal on the forest trail.

Crystal tore off the hat, hair splaying this way and that.

"Sweet," Grant said.

She slid onto a bar stool and picked up the powerful hair dryer. She leered at Grant, penciled eyebrow raised.

"My sister visits some," he said. "She indoctrinated me as to what was and was not an adequate hair dryer for a woman."

"Cool. I met your neighbor. He was impressed you had a girl staying with you."

Grant turned from the stove. "Do you mean he thought I was gay?"

"Hey, I don't know … He seemed like a pretty sensitive guy."

"Be real, Frank? He wouldn't know sensitive if it licked him on the neck."

"Ooh … does that happen around here much?"

"Look, you've had a good night's sleep. Your hair looks and smells really nice. So be careful baiting a man who is sleep-deprived and hasn't had female companionship since his residency."

Deep pools of sparkling amber gazed at him. He had no doubt she could see deep inside him. His lustful desires, need for intimacy and rescue. Grant broke the stare and then regretted it. He looked back. The pools deepened, drawing him in. He reached out and picked up her hand—soft, tender, and yet steady. "You're a beautiful woman, Crystal. I would have been honored to have you share my home in other circumstances. Perhaps when this is all over, we could give it another start."

Crystal breathed deeply. She let him hold her hand and then placed her hand over his. "You were in the room with me last night?"

The question hit him like ice water to the face. She did know. Had she been awake? No she wasn't, of that he was certain. "I was," he said, unwilling to go further.

"What happened?"

Grant pulled his hand from Crystal's. He turned to the stove and rotated the gas knob to off. Dropping his head, he exhaled slowly, shuddering ever so slightly. *Don't get involved,* his mind told him. It was too soon.

"Were you checking or scouting the location for security? Or was it something personal involving me? Was it the war?"

What was she talking about? What did she sense that made her think this all had to do with Afghanistan? The salty smell of cooking grease and crackle of bacon collided with uncertainty as he fought to collect his thoughts. He put down the spatula and walked around the counter, sitting next to Crystal. How could he explain?

He didn't know what to say.

Hesitantly he again reached for her hand, cradled it, and examined her clean well-trimmed fingernails as he took slow deep breaths. Searching for answers anywhere they'd come from.

•

It had been a simple question. She didn't expect any earth-shattering revelation of voyeurism or sexual perversion. What she'd gotten was a flood of sentiment from a man incapable of opening his heart to another human being, male or female. Was he unable to make a meaningful connection, self-absorbed like an autistic? Or was the real Grant a loving and warm man beaten down by the inhumanity of war and struggling for normalcy?

Crystal felt a suffocating tightness. Grant—anxiously hungering for air. Though she had only known him a few days, the need to reach out to him was powerful. But would it help? She had to try. "Grant, I have no idea what happens to men during war. I've seen it wreak havoc on some of the young men of my tribe. It's devastated you too. Have you ever gotten therapy?"

He exhaled as if an elephant had sat on his chest. Closed his eyes and shook his head. "I'm a physician, Crystal, there are men … patients much more traumatized than I was."

"What happened over there?"

He looked to the phone and then out the window to the bay. Searching for something or someone to interrupt and free him from this confrontation.

Crystal placed her hands on either side of his head, fixed his pained and disturbed gaze—moist eyes but no tears. "Have you ever told anyone about what happened to you over there?"

His head shook weakly. "No."

"Will you tell me?"

When he nodded, a tear rolled down his cheek. "I lost most of my squad in an attack outside Kandahar."

Crystal removed her hands from entrapping his head and picked up the closest hand. There was strength and resolve in his touch. But behind a curtain of haze she perceived a man groping ineffectively.

"I'm a physician. I carried only a handgun for personal protection. The Special Forces with me had M-16s and grenade launchers. We were in a Humvee coming back from a medivac when we hit an IED." His eyes darted back and forth, reliving the events. Pain gripped her. "The vehicle ended up on its side and one of the Special Forces guys, Henderson, was killed outright. Two more were injured pretty bad so that just left me and Mac MacDonald. We were pinned down and reinforcements were half an hour away." His palm was clammy. He looked away and swallowed hard. She wasn't sure he would continue.

Gently she rubbed her hand up and down his forearm. The skin felt weathered, the hairs soft and pleasant. But the muscles underneath were taut and ready to fight. When he looked back she gave him a reassuring nod.

"MacDonald threw me one of the M-16s and he started lobbing grenades with the launcher. I had to cover him each time he exposed himself to launch. We were holding our own." His head dropped and shook side to side. His chest heaved with short shallow breaths. "They were just kids and a woman … but they had kaloshnikoffs and they meant to finish us off before the helicopters got there." He stared out the window. Time stood still.

The phone rang.

Grant reluctantly pulled away from Crystal and answered it. He listened for about a minute and then said, "Right, in the conference room at one o'clock. I'll be there."

Squeaking came from the phone.

He said, "You want Miss Blackrock also, and her grandfather if he can make it."

Crystal nodded.

"Right, we'll do what we can."

He hung up and turned the frying pan back on. "I guess we better get to breakfast. Did you decide what you'd like?"

"French toast would be great." Crystal came around the breakfast bar and stood behind him. She wrapped her arms around him, felt his strong haunches against her abdomen, held tight for support. "What happened?"

He broke three eggs, hesitated, and began beating them. "I killed the woman and at least one of the insurgents. Mac was hit in the head about the fourth or fifth grenade he launched, dead immediately. We got the other two out. Lieutenant Frost lost a leg and part of his bowel. Sergeant Grimes lost a few fingers, busted some ribs, and ended up with a plate in his skull." Grant swallowed hard. "I got a decoration." He choked as his head dropped and a shudder ran up his spine.

Crystal held tight. The shaking stopped. She ran her hands up and down his arms, hoping to impart some measure of understanding but at the same time being overwhelmed by the proximity of his manhood.

"For killing women and children," he choked out.

Crystal turned Grant to face her, fighting back tears. The hurt he felt encompassed them both, bound them in a powerful grip that ached for compassion, understanding, and more. She couldn't take the suffering away from Grant Sands, but the healing had begun. "Thank you for telling me." She pulled his head down with both hands and gently kissed his forehead.

Standing perfectly still, Grant accepted her support and consolation. "That's what I did," he said.

"You did what you had to do. They'd have killed all of you … you—"

"I mean, that's what I did last night in the bedroom. I kissed your forehead, not sure why. I guess it was just the whole situation. I'm sorry … There's a lock on the door. I won't be offended if you choose to use it tonight."

Crystal laughed. "To protect me from the dreaded forehead kisser?"

Grant smiled, rolled his eyes, and nodded slightly.

Crystal replaced her hands on his head, gently kissed his nose and slipped down to his mouth. Sensitive lips transmitted a tingling to her ears and scalp. Her heart fluttered, or was that Grant's? She parted the kiss after longer than she'd first intended. His eyes opened. "You're a good man, Grant. You just need a little cultivating and loving care."

"From you?" he asked, eyebrows raised.

"I'm capable," Crystal scolded. "Let's get through this, and then we'll see if you are really the man my grandpa thinks you could be."

"So, he likes me."

Crystal raised her eyebrows.

Chapter 30

Grant Sands' Master Bedroom

The ache in Crystal's body confused her. At first she'd thought it was the suffering that Grant had experienced in Afghanistan. But now back in the bedroom she thought it was more like the muscle fatigue she'd felt after weeping for hours the night of her mother's fiery car crash so many years ago.

Crystal's mother was late getting home to the farm that night. She'd been late before, had run-ins with the law. But she'd always made it home, eventually. And, she'd been getting better.

Just after dusk a phone call had left her grandmother sobbing at the kitchen table. Her grandfather, the color drained from his face, grabbed his truck keys and grim-faced stumbled out the door.

Crystal followed him onto the porch. She'd watched as the old pickup veered through the farm yard and down the dirt road.

"Stop, Grandpa!" She'd yelled after the skidding truck and dust cloud.

In the distance, down by the county road, smoke billowed from a ball of fire nearly hidden by dense trees. The setting sun to the west left eerie shadows across the moss-covered cypresses that bordered the swamp.

Brake lights on the truck blinked as her grandfather accelerated out of a stand of trees, dust off the dry road obscuring his next turn. Crystal ran after him. She'd run down to the paved road countless times to meet her mother, never knowing the mood she'd find the suffering woman in—a single mother, abandoned by Crystal's father, drug addicted and homeless, except for her parents' farm.

She pushed the burn in her thirteen-year-old lanky legs to the back of her mind and dug her hiking boots into the gravel-covered road up to the damp green pasture. At the crest of the hill she recognized the smoldering wreck in the distance—her mother's rusted Mustang. Nose down in the ditch perched on its side, crumpled nearly unrecognizable.

She'd probably screamed, she didn't really remember. But she did remember the dreadful spasm that gripped her stomach and tried to pull her heart up through her throat.

Her head pounded as she reached the side of her grandfather's truck. Two Sheriffs' cars sat off the side of the asphalt with flashing blue and red lights. A fire truck roared down the two-lane road, squealing to a stop as the flames swirled into a sickening mix of black smoke, burning rubber and death.

Her grandfather took her hand and stepped behind the old farm truck as helmeted and heavily clad fireman directed a stream of water onto the burned-out carcass that most certainly held her mother.

"She's burning, Grandpa," she'd said.

His grip tightened. "They're doing everything they can, Crystal," he said, glancing at her but then looking to the setting sun. A single tear escaped the corner of his eye.

"Is she … dead?" Crystal had asked as if someone else was asking the question—not the immature adolescent girl of a downtrodden single mother. It was the voice of the level-headed honor student that her grandmother had initiated the previous year to the ways of the Creek healers. She was old enough, her grandmother had said, to study the ancestral healing art, mature enough to help the sick and dying to connect with nature. And above all, she was still pure enough to be open to the teaching of the spirits, of the Creator.

She didn't feel old or mature that day. Heat off the twisted inferno crept into her soul, and the dancing light painted ghostly landscapes across her grandfather's sunburnt face. Cows lazily drank from the long metal trough near the dirt access road, oblivious to the life-changing event the other side of their range fence.

Her grandfather turned her toward him and bent just enough to be at eye level. "We'll get through this, Crystal—you, Grandma, and me. It'll take awhile … and I'm not saying it won't hurt but we will get through it, Sweetie."

She'd tried to nod her trembling head but just wet her lips and whispered, "Okay, Grandpa." Sorrow beyond belief gripped her and even though only thirteen she'd known life would never again be simple and innocent.

Chapter 31

Medical Staff Conference Room, Community Medical Center

"Why would a terrorist risk exposing himself to you at the hospital?" Agent Sandra Meyers of the FBI asked. She was nearly a head shorter than Grant but moved about the conference room with a Napoleonic air, mid-level high heels clicking in quick bursts. Three members of Homeland Security clustered about the other end of the conference table, taking notes and fidgeting with a video machine.

"Look, we've been through this. Yes, I did have dealings with Pakistani and Afghan physicians during the war. I will review your photo file but I had never seen Dr. Abdul Patel before." He'd been through this same course of questioning earlier with Sheriff Tumley. It was nearly four o'clock, his neck and ears warmed with the flush of frustration.

He was about to launch into his reassessment of the shooting incident when Crystal and her grandfather were shuffled into the room.

Agent Meyers made introductions.

Grant stood and placed an arm around Will Blackrock. "The leg doing okay?"

"Better than my heart," Blackrock said. "Murderers! And now they are after my granddaughter." He tossed his crutch into a chair and raised both hands to the ceiling. "Guide us ancient ones. Restore nature's harmony and lead home the wandering spirits."

Crystal patted her grandfather's shoulder. He rotated his palms up and peered into them, awaiting an answer.

She wrapped her hands around Grant's free arm. "Have you had a break? Can I get you some coffee or something?"

Did he look that bad? "We won't have you all much longer, Miss Blackrock," Agent Meyers answered. "This is mostly a technicality for you and your grandfather. Policy is to at least eyeball all the principals in an investigation." Tired eyes shifted from Crystal to Will Blackrock. "We have your statements from Sheriff Tumley, and I don't think we'll need any more. Doctor Sands has given us everything he can recall and will review our photo files later tonight or tomorrow morning."

The Homeland Security team started picking up their folders and preparing to leave.

"So formally, Miss Blackrock, do you or your grandfather have anything to add, anything new you might have remembered?"

"Nothing, you've got everything I can think of," Crystal answered. "Grandpa, anything?"

Will Blackrock grunted and rubbing his jaw glanced at Agent Meyers and then back to Grant. "For lack of a better term for your reports ... I meditated last night."

Where was this going? The flushing extended up the back of Grant's neck. Crystal gave her grandfather a stern gaze. The Homeland Security team stopped picking up papers.

Will Blackrock pulled a small ring-binder from his pocket. "At the river that first evening, there were three maybe four men out in the woods. One was an Arab and one was dark skinned, Hispanic maybe. This one had a scarred ear ... probably not from birth. Looked like a burn or battle injury."

"You saw them that night, enough to make an ID?" Agent Meyers asked.

"Something like that," Will said. "I couldn't tell anything about the others."

"Could you identify them from a photograph?" Meyers asked.

"I never saw their faces."

"Did you actually see these features you are describing to us?"

"Perhaps not as you see, Agent Meyers, but every bit as clearly, maybe even more clearly."

"Now what do you mean by that?" She put both hands on the conference table and leaned toward Will.

"Agent Meyers, this should be valuable information," Grant interceded. "Along with the vehicle description and where they're headed. They are all parts to the puzzle, reliable parts. Who cares how you come about the information?"

Meyers looked up into Grant's stare. Long black eyelashes veiled penetrating pupils framed by a ring of chocolate brown. The lids blinked and she flopped into a chair, crossing nylon clad legs. "Okay, I'll include it in the report. Can't be any worse than the stuff we get from the field in the Far East, or from some of the local police forces."

Grant decided to leave the discussion there. Fight the battles you can win.

◆

They settled her grandfather back into his hospital room and then retraced their circuitous street route back to the Country Club, with a few variations.

"Thank you for defending my grandfather today," Crystal said once they were back in the townhouse. "He would not have challenged the agent ... out of respect, you understand."

"I do. I think Agent Meyers saw that eventually," Grant said.

"Always the diplomat, Dr. Sands." She chuckled.

Grant slid into the kitchen and grabbed cups out of the cupboard. "If we heat some tea, and hurry, I think we can catch the sunset off the dock."

"Trying to impress your neighbor with your heterosexuality?" She giggled. God, she was acting like a school girl!

Grant pointed at her and dropped his thumb like the hammer of a gun.

Crystal grabbed her chest. "A dangerous, murderous heterosexual."

"Yeah, right," he said as he turned to the microwave.

She called to check on her grandfather while Grant prepared the tea. "Grandpa, we'll be out back of Grant's townhouse for a few minutes, if you need anything, I have my cell phone. Okay?"

"He likes you," her grandfather said.

Her spirit lightened and warmth wrapped her core.

"Oh, you already knew that! You are a smart girl, my granddaughter."

"Grandpa, hold your tongue. I am a guest in this man's home. Let's not make things any more difficult than they already are." She placed a finger over her lips and blew a "shhh" into the mouthpiece.

"Follow your heart, Crystal, don't think so much." He always used her christened name when he wanted to impart grown-up advice. He'd done it since she was a teenager.

"Rest well, Grandpa. I'll figure it all out."

Grant stood with the back door open, teacups in hand. She accepted one. The aroma of hot honey and tangy lemon teased her senses.

"Is that okay?" Grant asked as she sipped from the steaming cup.

"Fine, and thank you for letting me stay another night. I hope it doesn't put you in anymore danger ... been enough already."

Grant studied her over the steam from his cup. "Thank you. No matter where this leads, this has been an eye-opening week for me."

She stepped out into the moist, coolness of the evening.

He offered his hand as they approached the dock. "There are definitely some loose ends the Sheriff and FBI need to tie-up. I'd be lying if I said I had no concerns."

Was he just being a gentleman, assisting the lady? Probably. Now she was over thinking. At the end of the dock, Grant set his cup on the railing and tentatively placed an arm around her waist, resting his hand on her hip. He looked down at her, asking permission with his eyes.

Crystal held his hand as they studied the setting sun. His firm thigh nestled against the curve of her buttock. Waves lapping the dock caused him to sway into her in a muted dancing movement. His grip on her tightened as he married the motion of their two bodies.

Fantasies of joined hips thrusting in rhythm melted her stomach, and a warmth rose up her spine. She took a long drink of tea, sweet but a bite of lemon. The parallel to her relationship with Grant tweaked her consciousness.

"How is your hip doing? You're not limping very much." She placed a hand on his chest and played with one of the buttons. It came undone by accident. She slid her hand onto the skin and chest hair underneath. Her fingers tingled as his muscle involuntarily tensed.

"It'll be fine. I do miss the special attention you gave the other night though." A smile creased his lip.

"Special attention for a special soldier," she said. "Do you make a habit of being a knight in shining armor? Or are my grandfather and me an exception to the rule?"

"An exceptional exception." He chuckled.

She pulled back and studied him. "Will it bother you if I set up a sacred site on the property? I could use the area next to the garage. Your neighbor is not tolerant of Indian activities being carried on in the backyard."

Grant tipped his head slightly.

"It's a long story," she said, turning again to catch the setting sun. She wrapped Grant's arms around her, as much for warmth as the obvious sensual connection. His loins molded pleasurably to her backside as they watched the sun slip into the horizon. Unexpectedly a content subtle moan escaped her lips. Grant's arms tightened and he lowered his mouth next to her ear. The lobe twitched as he gently nudged it with his lips. Nerve endings sizzled. She fought to stay still.

"Do you think there is any chance for us, Crystal?"

Did he really say that? She was sure he had. Her breath caught. The blood in her neck boiled. She dared not move, dared not challenge the fragility of the moment. Then her legs shifted slightly and she gently thrust her buttocks back into Grant's firm maleness. The animalistic response answered his question.

"I feel things I thought were gone forever …"

She turned to him and placed a finger over his lips. "We are from different worlds, Grant." It was what her mind told her, but her heart raced and private areas warmed. "I'm not saying no. It's complicated. Even our healing beliefs are in conflict. Could you ever accept that … should I even ask you to accept what is just not in your nature?"

"I might be a whole lot more flexible than you think."

"You'd have to be."

"Look, Crystal, I'm not insensitive to the beliefs and practices of the Creek and other tribes—"

"It's not the same. Living here in a country club atmosphere doesn't exactly lend itself to close communing with nature, the plants and the trees." Crystal spread her arm across the windswept bay waters and up the grass-covered bluff to the south.

"They've done what they can to live in harmony with nature and the past," Grant countered.

"Yeah, I got that from your neighbor this morning."

"Frank! He doesn't know anything about the area or its heritage." He removed his arms from Crystal and followed her gaze to the ancient oaks that dominated the top of the bluff. His head shook back and forth.

Was she being too hard on him? Could she change ... move to town ... live in a country-club condo under sparkling skies, along the windswept banks of the bay? Live with Grant?

She put a hand on his shoulder. Piercing grey-blue eyes beckoned her to consider the alternatives. To what ... compromise her Creek birthright and obligations? Could they really find a common ground, a calculated middle-of-the-road that would satisfy both of them?

She sensed frustration. "Hey, how about a truce." Crystal chortled. "This is all getting much too serious for such a beautiful sunset."

Grant picked up her hand and kissed it, warm lips lingering along the smooth recesses. When he glanced up, his blue eyes sparkled. Her heart pounded and a flush surged into her cheeks. This was a man worth saving, and loving. But she was uneasy.

The orange hue of the setting sun teased the underside of clouds far off to the west. Then a quick succession of colors raced about the clouds and finally settled on the distant horizon—first bronze, then aquamarine green, and finally a fading blue. Her grandfather was right about this sacred ceremonial bluff, the sunrise and sunset would both be visible throughout most of the year.

Grant held her lightly as day faded to night. Confident hands rested on her shoulders stoking a spirit of subtle sanguinity. A force was at work on the bluff beyond Grant's powerful masculinity. It was the creeping presences of her ancestors, intent on drawing them, as a couple, on an uncharted spiritual journey. Unmistakably, the ancients wanted her and Grant together. And they wanted them here, on the bluff.

Chapter 32

FBI Office Panama City

Agent Meyers arranged for Grant to review the terrorist photos at the downtown FBI office that evening. When Grant arrived, near eight o'clock, she and Sheriff Tumley stood face to face.

"Yeah, well, it's a little different down here, lady." Sheriff Tumley poked a pudgy finger in the chest of the diminutive FBI agent.

"It's not just about the South, Sheriff," Meyers countered, pushing a messy pile of paper out of the way to make room for her coffee cup. "You can chew your tobacco until cow shit freezes. But if we don't find this terrorist in the next forty-eight hours, we may as well pack it in." She turned to Grant as he entered and flipped a hand toward Tumley as if she were swatting a bothersome fly.

The terrorist files had been downloaded from Washington. It took Grant less than an hour sitting at the archaic computer monitor to give them a thumbs down. It was a joke, most of the pictures showed men with full beards. "Patel was nearly clean shaven. Most of these … you can't see half the face." Grant closed the last computer screen. "I really think the guy was more a blackmail victim than a terrorist. He spoke excellent English. I'll bet he did some medical training in the United States or Great Britain. You might find him in records of surgical residencies."

"That might take overtime work," the Sheriff chided.

Grant rose to leave as Agent Meyers glared at Tumley.

A slim, younger man with rolled-up shirtsleeves and tie askew leaned close to Meyers and whispered in her ear.

She tilted her head. A twitch briefly strained the corner of her mouth. She turned away from Tumley's examining eyes. "The FBI has the lead on this ... but we're domestic, mostly."

The younger agent screwed his mouth slightly and returned to the terrorist files.

"I can access U. S. medical staff files. But for foreign files we'll need to go through the State Department or CIA." She pointed at the other agent, who was already typing at the computer keyboard. "Make it happen, Carl."

Tumley, rolling his eyes, held the door open for Grant. A low whistle escaped the Sheriff's lips as they left the unnervingly silent command center.

Cross put him through the evasion protocol once again and by ten o'clock he was back in the Country Club. He parked the Jeep next to the garage so he could drive his corvette if the opportunity arose. He was careful to avoid the orange-tape fence that delineated the Indian burial site just west of his residence. The "Indian stuff" his neighbor had referred to when confronting Crystal.

She had certainly gotten her feathers in a wad over that affair. He understood though, native heritage was not important to the majority of Americans who traced their ancestry back to Europe. The burial grounds near his home appeared mixed in origin, Creek but some Cherokee and maybe other tribes too. The particulars still needed more investigating.

His townhouse construction had been moved forty feet east to avoid the sacred site. The city and state would ultimately decide the fate of the plot. Grant looked out over the beat-down mounds—peaceful beneath majestic oaks—bathed in moonlight with a dusting of stars. They knew how to pick an eternal resting place.

Apparently they also knew how to dress gunshot wounds. His hip was healing well and Will Blackrock showed no signs of infection in his wound. Certainly the Creeks, over the centuries, had made some discoveries of natural healing. Not scientific though, and as Crystal amply pointed out, native healers were not interested in trying to prove what time immortal had bestowed upon them. It was as much an acceptance of faith as any modern religion.

•

The knock on the bedroom door interrupted an enchanted, spiritual awareness that Crystal had been assimilating for nearly an hour. She literally ached from the experience. "Come in," she answered.

Grant opened the unlocked door. "Just me, the depraved forehead kisser."

Crystal unwound her legs and pulled the bed-covers up as Grant entered. "How did it go?"

"Keystone Cops, I'm afraid. They're looking in the wrong places."

"They're concentrating on the terrorist angle?" Crystal asked and brushed a string of hair behind her ear.

"Exactly. And, to me, most of the terrorists look alike. Or have beards that make them unrecognizable."

"You still think he's an actual practicing doctor from Pakistan, maybe a surgeon?" She sat up in the bed.

He nodded. "I do."

"Certainly Homeland Security can get file photos of physicians at hospitals in that region." She tipped her head to the side. "Waziristan right?"

"Yeah, the mountains of northern Pakistan. They call the area Waziristan."

"There can't be but a few hospitals around there that have surgical capabilities." She pulled the covers back and stood up, showing bare legs. "Let's Google large cities in Waziristan."

Ten minutes later they had identified no more than six cities in the mountainous Waziristan region that might be large enough for a major hospital. Crystal climbed back on the bed triumphantly.

Grant folded their notes and put them in his pocket. "I just need a few things for the night. Your grandfather doing okay?"

"He's fine. Any thing on the local side?"

Grant rubbed his eyes and chin. "No, the FBI seems focused on Doctor Patel and I think Sheriff Tumley has hit some walls when it comes to vehicle ID and likely candidates."

"He could be right in front of them," Crystal said. She'd continued to search her mind for any reasonable connections. "You know, the local connection to the smugglers may be more Islamic terrorist oriented than criminal smuggling ... Do you think that's being taken into account?"

"Honestly, with the grilling on Patel, I haven't thought a lot about what the motivations of the local accomplice would be ... but I think you're on the right track. Could be either and neither should be discounted."

Crystal crossed her legs conscious of her near nakedness.

Grant hesitated. "The deputy up the road gave me a thumbs up when I passed. So … I guess we're in the clear so far."

"Great. I hope it stays that way."

Grant stepped nearer to the bed. What was he doing? Did he want to climb in with her? She hadn't thought of that prospect. Certainly that wasn't his intent, was it?

"Did your grandfather actually see the smugglers?" Grant asked.

"Oh, probably," Crystal said. "You know we see lots of things that are never really remembered. I think it became clear when he was able to cleanse his mind and connect better with his memory. That's not a real good explanation for the FBI though."

"Well, information is information."

Crystal adjusted the scrub top she had scored from Grant's dresser. It tended to creep down and expose a bit more than Grant might be ready for, though he should be ready for it after five years. That was his last relationship. That was how he had termed it, didn't say anything about one-night stands or flings. Could a man really go five years without sex?

"Is that some attempt to mix the new with the ancient?" Grant asked, looking at Crystal like a biology specimen, examining her breathing, her bare legs.

"You mean my meditation and the scrub top, cute huh?" She held out her arms for his inspection. "I didn't want to use anything you might have an attachment to … you aren't attached to this scrub top are you?"

"And what if I was?"

"So you want it back, is that what you're saying." She grinned. "Does that mean the mad forehead kisser is gonna take it back if I don't do it voluntarily?"

"No, no, nothing like that," he said, sitting on the edge of the bed. "We can talk about it."

"So you think you can talk the shirt off my back. Is that it?"

"I would never take advantage of a guest in my home." His eyes sparkled as he leaned toward her.

This shouldn't be happening. She was as much to blame as he was. She kept encouraging him, teasing and tempting.

Fire jumped in his eyes as he struggled to hold her gaze. The scrub top crept lower as her breathing deepened. His eyes lost the battle and gave in to the temptation of her breasts as the V-top revealed more and more of her cleavage. Air flushed through Grant's nostrils, his teeth ground nearly imperceptibly, yet he held steady.

She picked up Grant's toughened hand and placed it on her bare chest, hugging it tightly. His look was of relief, not surprise, not excitement. His other hand stroked her hair and rested softly on her cheek. The taste buds in the back of her throat flared as if she'd taken a spoonful of honey. It expanded and warmed into her ears and shoulders.

"You are a beautiful woman, Crystal." His voice was low and husky.

His fingers touched her mouth, tracing the edges. Her tongue moistened the silky roll of her lips involuntaril —too fast. She had to consider her heritage, the spiritual ability of her offspring. It was never easy. Her grandparents had both made that clear. She was confused and scared. Her body wanted this man, wanted to feel his hands caressing her, feel the power of his body.

"Grant … Grant …"

She leaned into his kiss and delicately nibbled at his tongue, which cautiously explored hers. Eyes closed, she felt butterflies traverse her bosom and abdomen. The embrace continued as Grant's weight bore down on her. She lay on his bed, in his arms. The symbolism was not lost on her. She did not take lightly the entanglement of emotions that gripped them, emotions that had brought them to this night of animalistic needs, which seemed beyond their control.

The scrub top was around her neck. Hummingbirds attacked her breasts as delicately as they extracted nectar from the goldenrod. Her hands coursed through Grant's unruly hair as he blessed the sensitive folds beneath her breast.

"This could be a mistake," she exhaled between pants.

He pulled back, smiling adorably. "In what way?"

She toyed with the hair above his ear—gazed over his head — searching for an explanation. "I'm no one-night stand, Grant … and I come with baggage."

His lips gently nibbled hers. He studied her. The kiss deepened as he circled and twisted his fingers through her hair.

She came up for air. "Grant … are you sure?"

He stopped kissing and looked down tenderly at her. "I know it's only been a couple of days, and pretty crazy days at that." He swallowed hard. "But Crystal you're the best thing that's ever happened to me. You've brought the light back into my life."

She rose up on an elbow and gazed into his blue-grey eyes. Feelings, intuition, and emotions, how did they all fit together? What was expected of her? What was the path she should take? Did that path include Grant? How could it?

He softly kissed her nose. "I have never felt this way about any other woman. You are truly my soul mate. Sure, the battles I've fought have left me scarred. But they've also shown me what is important and worthwhile."

She melted into his embrace, held his simmering chest tightly, and stroked the taut depths of his shoulders and back. She wrapped herself around him—protective and united—tingling and welcoming.

Crystal was amazed at the patient, gentle caresses delivered with tender respect. Strong hands cradled, molded, and guided her to the meadow of peace and contentment.

Grant lay behind her, embracing her as they drifted off to sleep. Visions of beloved ancestor and animals of the forest flickered through Crystal's subconscious, all in pairs. All looked upon her with knowing and loving gazes, accepting.

•

Crystal held his arm firmly against her breasts as she slept, stirring infrequently. Grant had positioned them on their left sides to take the pressure off his injured hip. Somewhere in the dark hours he awoke to the subtle pressure of Crystal's buttocks against him. He felt her regular breaths against his chest through the girlish musculature of her back.

Engulfed in her womanhood, he reveled in her purity, the pleasing rise and fall of her ribs and abdomen. How long they lay he had no idea. But the firestorm that was Crystal Blackrock slowly worked its way to his core. She was a force of nature beyond his comprehension. Yet here she was in his bed, searching along with him for understanding and connection.

Her skin felt like flower petals beneath his weathered hands, the contrast as stark as their lives. A low murmur came from the darkness and her body stiffened. Her breathing became irregular.

She threw back the covers and turned into his arms. He imagined in the darkness her eyes staring at him.

"It might be dangerous for either of us to get too used to this," she whispered. A long sigh escaped her lips as she eased her head onto his shoulder, the wetness of a tear tore into his heart.

What was he getting into? What did the future hold?

Chapter 33

Agent Meyers was no further along in the investigation than the previous night. Papers strewn over several desks mixed with empty coffee cups and breakfast wrappers, a busy night of law enforcement. The Bay County offices of the FBI looked a far cry from the sterile efficiency the agency generally portrayed.

"It's not hard. You concentrate on the eyes ... how far apart they're spread." Meyers, probably in her late thirties, pointed at pictures of known terrorists and drug traffickers. "You know, the hair line and the set of the lips. Try to ignore the beards."

Grant glared at the agent as he would a pestering vagrant on a street corner. "He's not here, I tell you. I really don't think he's a career terrorist."

"I know, I know. He's a respected Pakistani physician." She threw her arms in the air. "All we need is a printout of British and American surgical residents from the past fifteen years ... and there he'd be! Right?"

The athletic well-proportioned Meyers paced back and forth across the conference room, high heels clicking. She stopped and drummed her fingers on the table. "Look, this is bad. I've got three reports of dead bodies and missing persons. At the south end of the Apalachicola Forest they found a dead man who'd obviously been in a shoot-out. His wife and thirteen-year-old daughter are missing."

Grant's stomach turned over. What would be the fate of those two women? He'd seen hopelessness in the faces of young Afghan women, trapped in a life not worth living. He breathed deeply and handed Meyers the list of Waziristan cities he'd shown her earlier.

"Okay, damn!" She turned to a clean-cut Ivy League kid who towered over her and poked a well-manicure turquoise fingernail against his monogrammed tie. "Retake the doctor's statement. This time get Pakistani hospitals and cities that our perp might have come from. And keep on State … tell them the files are the highest priority."

Tight-lipped, the young agent said nothing.

Grant did like the woman. She'd played the party line long enough, now it was time for some initiative. This was probably how she'd gotten where she was with the FBI, played by the rules but thought outside the box when necessary.

"You're free to go when Simpson finishes with your statement, Doctor Sands." She flipped her black curly hair and smiled through straight white teeth.

"I'll be off the rest of the week," Grant said. "Do you need me to come back tomorrow or later today?"

Meyers rubbed two fingers across her forehead as she studied swaying palm trees out the window. "No. The more you're moving in and out of town, the more likely your location will be compromised. You sit tight and we'll bring what we get out to your townhouse."

Grant leaned back in the office chair. "Anything on their local accomplice?" he asked.

She turned, tight lipped. "Not that I know of. Sheriff Tumley is still working it … I wish there was something we could do to help."

•

Crystal finally stirred as the morning sun beat through the window blinds. Grant was gone. He'd probably showered in the guest bathroom. She hadn't heard a sound.

She took her time in the large glass and tile master shower, lathered and soaped intimate areas that had unmistakably awakened the previous night. She lingered as warm water coursed through her hair, rinsing away the scent that was Grant. What had come over her? Did she really expect this wounded veteran to abandon his beliefs? Follow her into the life of a Creek husband and father? Was it even possible?

She finished toweling off, rummaged through her overnight bag, applied her toiletries, and settled on jeans and an earth-toned blouse.

On the way out of the subdivision, she waved at a Sheriff's deputy she did not recognize and pumped the gas pedal of the pickup truck to keep it from stalling.

At the hospital, her grandfather stood fully dressed, looking out a window to the east. He turned and smiled as she entered, raised his cup of coffee in salute.

"Hey, you're up and at it I see," she said. "How's the leg this morning?"

"Limbering up a bit. How was your night?"

He knew something. It had always been that way. But he respected her privacy and asked only to make sure she was okay. "More exciting than yours, I'm sure."

She rolled her eyes and poured coffee from a pot on his breakfast tray into a Styrofoam cup sitting on the bedside-stand.

Her grandfather continued to look to the east. "I saw the sunrise this morning, and I imagined how the sunset must look from the bluff."

"Oh, it was wonderful, Grandpa. I saw it last night when Grant and I were on the dock."

"Catching sunsets with him now?" His face glowed with an impish grin.

Crystal held her cup of coffee and let the steam bathe her face. The warmth worked its way into her shoulders. Contentment blossomed in her chest as she thought of her night with Grant and of the words he had spoken to her. Could it be real? Did they have a chance?

She looked at her grandfather, the only parent she'd known throughout her adult life. "What am I going to do, Grandpa?" She walked to the window and leaned her head against his firm shoulder.

"At some point, Crystal, you'll have to let go. Let the spirits guide you, give your heart to a man, your soul to your children. It's not easy, but when the time comes it will seem natural. You would not be able to imagine life any different."

"It doesn't feel so straightforward right now." She rubbed her cheek against the taut muscles beneath his denim shirt. "In fact, from where I'm standing everything looks like overgrown curves and corners."

His arm encircled her and rocked her as he'd done since she was a baby. It would work out, as it always had, as the spirits of her ancestors intended.

"You look like you're all set to go," she said.

"Signed the paperwork an hour ago."

Deputy Cross was at the truck when Crystal wheeled her grand-father into the parking lot.

"Back to Doctor Sands' house?" he asked.

"That's what the Sheriff wants. I think it is terribly imposing on Grant though," Crystal said.

She followed Cross's route once again, this time quite circu-itous. Was he just messing with her?

She settled her grandfather into the guest room as Grant had instructed. A third bedroom had been converted to an office. Grant would sleep on the family room fold-out couch. He had yet to return from the FBI offices.

"Ready to stretch your legs some? I can show you the bluff," Crystal said, as she eased the sliding-glass door open to the back-yard and the bay.

"Hand me that cane over there. I think I can manage."

With the aid of the cane and Crystal's arm they gingerly got to the dock. Her grandfather settled himself on a wooden bench and examined the bluff. He turned his head this way and that, taking in the sweet aromas of the magnolia trees and the dampness of the nearby wetlands. The wind rustled through his long graying hair and whipped across his craggy face in a lazy dance.

He nodded and smiled at Crystal. "This is the sacred place I have heard the elders speak of." He pointed to a raised area be-yond Grant's townhome where century-old oaks posed with veils of Spanish moss. "From that sacred ground the mating of the sun and moon has been observed for many eons."

"Mating … what are you talking about?"

"The sun can be continually observed from this bluff, from sunup to sunset." He waved his arm in an arch through the sky. "Every eighteen years the moon causes a total eclipse of the sun. The sacred male and female of Creek ancestry join as one in space … a truly memorable and magic time for our people."

Crystal followed her grandfather's gaze to a flock of pelicans navigating toward the Gulf. An observant osprey circled high above the bluff before settling at the top of an aging loblolly pine whose roots were lapped by the encroaching bay waters.

"Why has the site been lost for so long? There must have been some markings or signs at one time," Crystal asked.

"Well, the Creek came to this area from Georgia." He shaded his eyes and looked to the southwest, where the bay wrapped around on its journey to the Gulf of Mexico. "Most of us thought the sacred site would be on one of the barrier peninsula or islands, facing the north to take in the entire transit of the sun. Never really thought of it being up here on the southern side of North Bay. Makes sense though."

Crystal nodded. "I have felt the presence and power of the creator very intensely here. I can't explain it … it's actually overwhelming."

"Yes, it's obvious." Her grandfather turned his head slightly, listening to the wind, or maybe something else.

"It's damp out here, Grandpa. We should be heading back in."

Crystal helped her grandfather across the grass and up the rise toward the back of the townhouse.

Grant's neighbor, Frank, slid open his glass door and wished them a good morning. Crystal made cursory introductions as she and her grandfather approached the complex. They continued moving toward Grant's door. She had no desire to engage the ignoramus in conversation.

"Thanks for being quiet last night. The wife slept like a baby," Frank said.

Crystal tightened her grip on Will's left arm and kept moving.

"Have you been doin' your ceremonies around the side by the site?" he continued, apparently unaware of Crystal's attempt to run away.

She stopped, as did her grandfather. "Site?" she asked.

"Yeah, the burial site, over next to the doc's place. That area with all the orange tape … over near the rise and the old oaks." He pointed around the side of Grant's garage. "I'm sure he wouldn't mind you going inside the tape."

"No, I was pretty busy last night," Crystal said. "Ceremonies will have to wait a while."

"Maybe you can give the doc some tips on how to go about getting those remains moved." He lowered his voice. "The County Commission seems all bound up about what can and can't be done."

"With moving the remains, you mean?" Crystal said, a sick feeling gnawing at her stomach.

Frank stepped onto his patio, placed work gloves on a table, and pointed toward the bluff next to the townhouses. "We need to get everything moved before the association can start diggin' the boat ramp."

"And how is the doctor involved?" Crystal asked, dreading the response.

"He's in charge of the homeowner's committee looking into the issue, supposed to come up with a solution." Frank shrugged. "It's been just sittin' there as long as I've been here. I don't know if they're making progress or not. Doc would know."

Crystal thanked him for the information, looked at her grandfather, holding her face as impassive as possible. Frank closed the sliding door.

"So ... it's a burial ground also," she said.

"Probably," her grandfather answered, his lips held tightly together.

Crystal rolled her eyes. "Let's take a look, Grandpa." She shifted to his opposite arm as he reversed directions and moved the cane to his left hand.

A slight depression east of Grant's garage led to a slow rise toward ancient live oaks. A distinctive mound blended into the bluff, clearly man-made. Stretched strategically around the sacred site was dirtied and stained orange construction tape. Wooden stakes, two of which were broken, held the perimeter line, leaving a rather disheveled appearance.

Her grandfather rubbed his jaw and let the wind buffet his hair. She fought to breathe as the air was sucked out of her lungs. "Really! A boat ramp?"

Her grandfather knelt and picked up a fistful of dirt. He studied the scattered blades of grass that had become dislodged, islands of green in a sea of dark black earth. Slowly he massaged the dirt about in his hands and presented his soiled fingers to the morning sun. "We will respect you, our honored kin. The traditions of the Creator and the rights of your spirits will be seen to. Trust in this."

"This can't happen, Grandpa. It will not happen." Crystal's

heartbeat pounded in her throat.

"It is not our land, Granddaughter."

"This may be the most sacred of Creek sites in the Econfina Region. We have to do something."

"The County would have to issue permits for a boat ramp and the Department of Environmental Protection has to give them a certificate as well. It's not surprising the site has sat for so long."

Crystal choked back tears, looked to the bay and back to the bluff. "Don't they have to get permission from the tribe as well?"

"If they know which tribe. Maybe the University in Tallahassee would know? They have authority over the Native sites in the panhandle."

"I'm going to check at the court house to see what has been filed." She turned and looked over the windy bay, a firm set to her jaw. "This is not gonna happen." Was she drawing a fighting line in the dirt, in Grant's backyard?

Her grandfather leaned on his cane.

Did he foresee the battle that would rage between Crystal and her possible lover? Was this the end of her and Grant before they even got started? Maybe it was all for the best. It was a stretch to begin with. What was she thinking? There would always be conflicts like this. Their worlds too far apart—different dimensions.

"Come on, Grandpa. It's windy out here. We need to keep you warm. Infection loves a cold wound."

"Will you talk with the doctor?"

"Once I get all the facts." She held her chin high into the wind. "I don't know how far along they are. He may have been working on it for years. It won't be easy changing his mind or this homeowner's association."

"Doesn't look like anyone has been on the site. I doubt they even know what they've got here."

"A great place for a boat ramp apparently." She smirked, shook her head. "Sh—"

Chapter 34

Sands' Townhouse, North St. Andrews Bay

Grant threw his keys on the counter. Rubbed his hand through his hair and studied Will Blackrock snoozing with the television controller in his hand. Where was Crystal? He poked his head in the bedroom. No. His fishing hat was gone, and so were his corvette keys. What was she up to?

Grant opened the door to the garage. Will Blackrock's old truck was the sole inhabitant. "Christ," he whispered under his breath as he closed the door, not quiet enough.

Will stirred. "You're back," the elderly Indian said.

"Right … " Grant rubbed a hand over the back of his neck. "It looks like Crystal has taken my car."

"Sorry," Will said. "She's hellbent on getting to the courthouse, thought the fishing hat, sunglasses, and your vehicle would let her get by the deputy down the way."

"It must have worked, he just waved at me as I drove in." Grant sat across from the medicine man. "What's she up to?"

"Trying to find out what's up with the burial grounds next to your garage."

"At the courthouse?"

"The guy next door, Frank I think, says you're pulling a permit to build a boat ramp through the site."

Grant exhaled hard through tight lips. "He doesn't know what he's talking about."

"Well, it's all cordoned off like there is some plan or something."

"Yeah, okay. I hope she doesn't get spotted."

"I doubt any traffickers will be showing up at the courthouse?"

Will said. "She tucked her hair under the hat and wore some jeans and one of your shirts, looked like some scrawny kid."

Grant massaged the muscles at the base of his neck and studied Will. "Did you get settled in okay?"

"Perfectly. And thank you for allowing us into your home."

"You're welcome." Grant smiled. "Does she always learn things the hard way?"

"There is no substitute for learning from experience." Will grimaced. "As long as it doesn't kill you." He pointed at Grant. "War excepted, of course."

"She's a wonderful woman, your granddaughter ... I find myself drawn to her in ways I have never felt before. It may sound corny, but she reminds me of my grandmother."

"She's on a rough, fog-shrouded road with no marker signs." Will uneasily rubbed his weathered chin.

"What does that mean?" Grant asked. "Isn't she destined to be a Creek Medicine Woman, like the rest of your ancestors?"

"That, but possibly much more." He leaned toward Grant. "The Creek need strong and insightful leaders to navigate the future just as much as any other society or nation." He leaned back. "She must find her way so that the Creek Nation can also find its way."

"Sounds pretty heavy."

Will nodded. "She must first find her heart and spirit." He held his palms skyward. "She has opened her heart, Grant. She is just afraid of what she sees, afraid of what she feels for you. She has to learn to trust the course our all-seeing ancestors have plotted for her, for both of you."

Heaviness settled on Grant, not a burden but a protective shroud, a shield against the dangerous world. "I will be there for her if she wants me." He hesitated. "If you approve and think her mother would have approved?"

"I trust the spirits of our ancestors. They know the way. They know your and Crystal's destiny. Why that is and how it will come about is certainly unclear. But trust this, when the time is right a bright future will be revealed." He stood and put a hand on Grant's shoulder.

Miraculously the torment of lost love and Afghanistan that he had carried for so many years seemed to dissipate into the Medicine Man's healing fingers.

"Treat her well and be honest with her, young man," Will said as he turned and limped back into the guest bedroom.

Grant opened the sliding back door and stepped out onto the patio. He gazed over the oak-covered bluff, shook his head. Will Blackrock had given his permission for Grant to woo his granddaughter. But where could this lead? How was he going to set it right?

◆

"I understand you don't have any permits." Crystal glared at the obese clerk who had abandoned his club sandwich to examine the development records spread strategically on his counter. "I just want to see if they've applied for a permit." She pointed to plot number thirty-seven of Country Club Estates on the survey in front of her.

"Nothing gets into my computer until a permit is issued, Ma'am," he said, licking his fingers disgustingly.

This was getting nowhere. Her frustration with the county records system was winding into her frustration with Grant, the lost warrior. He was letting the idiotic homeowner's association destroy the most sacred site in all of the Bay area. For what? A damned boat ramp. To think she'd ever considered a possible future with him.

Her mind wandered—the firm guiding touch of his hands, warmth against her naked chest, pale blue eyes examining her deeply. He would have been a dedicated father, caring and attentive. She closed her eyes and shook her head from side to side. Anger, lust, and hope all crashed together as she fought to regain control. *Damn it, Crystal, you are no different from your mother.*

No! That was not true. She would not let herself fall into that deep pit of self loathing and depression. Her life would mean something. She would leave more than a pitifully shy and lonely little girl when she left this world.

"And I have to know what name the permit was applied under, and the month, before you can pull them and check."

Crystal looked at the notes she had scribbled on a folded newspaper.

"Actually, you'll need to check that with Mrs. Clemmons in contracting and planning," he said, shrinking back from the counter as if he expected Crystal to swat him with the paper.

"Back to Eleventh Street across from the library you mean?"

Crystal said through clenched teeth. She slowly exhaled through her nose, trying mostly in vain to control her urge to pound on the counter in frustration.

"They'll be closed for lunch now, Ma'am, till one-thirty." This time he clearly took a step back from the counter.

Crystal nodded. She would have to confront Grant. The only other option would be to find the homeowners' or the County Commission minutes and sift through them. That could take weeks and still could be a dead-end.

She dreaded the thought of what this would do to her and Grant. He was vulnerable. He'd just begun to open up and now she was going to come at him with both fists flying. Could she see her way past this? Could she just let the community tear her ancestors out of their sacred resting place and send them to some remote swamp or worse yet, a museum?

A sour taste rose in her throat as she stood outside the records building. It was turning bad. Just like all her other relationships. She'd once again picked the bad apple.

"Throw it back, Crystal." That's what her grandmother had always told her. "Keep looking. There are good apples out there, no point settling for a rotten one."

Grant couldn't be a "bad apple." He hadn't been that way, helping her and her grandfather, opening his home to them. Looks could be deceiving though. Once you start peeling sometimes you found things you weren't ready for. Like a worm, a festering disease that ruins the whole fruit. There certainly were worms in Grant's soul. Was this defiling of her people's sacred site the atrocity that would ruin everything?

She could deal with his self hatred, spawned from his war experience. There were ways to heal those wounds, might even leave him a better person, a better physician, husband, and father. Oh, Grant! For all the potential, she could not stomach a man who would despicably disregard the harmony of her ancestor's afterlife.

She didn't know that. She wasn't being fair. It wasn't like she'd caught him selling sacred artifacts or digging in a burial mound. They'd met on a hiking trail in a national forest! She'd stupidly made bad choices in the past. Flying off in a tirade wouldn't help, this time could be different. She needed to give him a fighting chance, as well as herself.

And it wasn't just the here and now. She'd glimpsed so much more that evening behind Grant's townhouse. The connection she felt with nature and her sacred heritage was extremely important —more so than anything that she might experience in her mortal life. Grant Sands was certainly a wonderful specimen of manhood with great potential. But he did have a lot of baggage.

She climbed into the Corvette and felt the power and rumble of the engine as she turned toward North Bay and Grant's townhouse. She enjoyed the throbbing vitality and responsiveness of the sports car. Her life should be like that. Unbridled energy, ready and waiting to be unleashed at the mere will of the operator. Why couldn't life and relationships be that easy?

Chapter 35

Sands' Townhouse

Deputy Cross gave her no more than a glance as she passed him on the way to the townhouse. Grant was kneeling near the burial site, talking with her grandfather as she drove up. He rose and handed a small fragment of pottery to the elder Indian, who wasn't as perturbed looking as Crystal thought he would be.

"Sorry I didn't check with you before I took your Corvette." She jabbed as she approached the two.

Her grandfather raised a graying eyebrow and glanced at Grant.

"I'm glad you're back safely." Grant set his jaw tightly and moved his mouth as if to speak.

Crystal tore off the hat and let her sticky hair blow about in the breeze. That seemed to disarm Grant as his scowl eased. It would be back soon enough! He wasn't going to like her questions.

"This looks like Cherokee stamping along the leading edge," her grandfather said as he turned back to Grant. "See the delicate cross hatching and a swirl etched just below it, that's typical Cherokee. Or, they may call it Mississippian in some of the journals. They really weren't called Cherokee or Creek until the 1500s."

"Yeah, in a lot of that time frame they were just called Woodland Indians." Grant examined the markings, facial muscles softening. "There are definitely some Creek buried here as well ... Swift Creek actually, I think."

"Three to five hundred years old then," her grandfather said.

"I'm not sure." Grant looked toward the blue-green bay. "There are some pieces from below the bluff that have an overlapping owl-eye, paddle stamp that is a characteristic of the later Creek."

Crystal pushed between the two and glared up at Grant. "How long have you known this was a burial site?" She pulled her tone just short of accusatory.

"Since I built the townhouse, a few years ago … turned up on the ground survey." Grant stepped back, tipped his head toward the oak trees on the bluff. "I expected there would be an artifact site here, with the rise of that bluff." He pointed northwest.

Crystal followed his finger. Moist, salty air pushed up the bluff from the marsh-covered bay. Majestic oaks stood silhouetted against small patches of clouds. Damp hair clung to the back of her neck adding to her irritation.

"It's the perfect site," her grandfather said. Slowly he presented his uplifted hands to the sky. He told Grant of the sacred nature of the bluff's location and the ability of worshiping ancestors to observe the sun continuously through the day.

Grant rubbed his chin as he listened intently.

"It allowed them to observe the sun and moon rising," he said. "Join the spirits in the sky and then return to Mother Earth."

"Like the owl," Crystal added. "It can also leave the ground and rise into the spirit world."

Grant was so in touch with the significance of the burial site. How could he play a role in its destruction? He probably just didn't understand the impact that moving her ancestors would have on the harmony of the area. As much as she didn't want to fight with him, she needed to stop this desecration.

Grant looked down at her as she shifted back and forth on her feet, a strong set to his mouth, likely an indicator of stubbornness and the battle to come. Distractingly, his large shirt sagged from her shoulders likely revealing a liberal amount of skin and cleavage. An approving twitch creased the side of his mouth. Focus. Sure he was a hunk of a man but there was so much more he needed to be.

Crystal laced her arm into her grandfather's. "It's a very big deal to move the remains of our Creek ancestors, you know." She looked at her grandfather, imploring him to be supportive. "The reburial process itself is exhausting and you have to find Creeks that are willing to be a part of the ceremony … for days."

A large black sedan turned into Grant's drive. Agent Meyers and a tall young man climbed out of the vehicle. Professionally, she scanned the tree-line to the south and the wind-blown bluff.

Looking back toward the hiking trail, she spoke into her phone. "We've got the house. Post up at the first cross-road. Let me know if we have any visitors." The unmarked vehicle eased from the bark-covered parking area, silently retracing the lone entrance road to the duplex.

Meyers punched the iPhone and dropped it casually into the pocket of a tailored suit top. The phone disappeared without so much as a bulge against her trim figure. No gun bulges either but Crystal knew she was carrying.

"Doctor Sands, Miss Blackrock." Meyers nodded toward Crystal's grandfather.

"To what do we owe the honor?" Grant asked.

"More photos for you to look at," Meyers said. "This time from the medical staffs at Peshawar, Dikhan, and Banu—Waziristan." She directed the younger agent, carrying a slim laptop, toward the townhouse. "Okay for us to go inside?"

"I need to get off my leg anyway," her grandfather said and followed the agent.

Grant shrugged and fell in behind them. The battle was postponed. Was she upset or not? The tightness in her stomach eased as she realized her face was flush. Whatever, might be good to let him stew over her comments for a while anyway? Maybe he'd come to a solution on his own without having to be browbeaten.

"We can send a car out to your farm to get some of your clothes, if you need," Meyers said.

At first Crystal wasn't sure what she was talking about until Meyers looked down at Grant's oversized shirt on her diminutive frame. "That won't be necessary, Agent," Crystal said.

"Fine." Meyers pursed her lips. "I guess it is kind of southeast rustic. Some men like that, I hear."

Crystal did not honor the crusty agent with a reply. She plopped the hat back on her head unceremoniously and followed the men into the house. Probably best not to point out that this was actually a disguise to avoid the deputy.

Grant settled at the dinner table as Meyers turned on the computer. Crystal re-examined her grandfather's leg in the guest bedroom. It was healing well, though he did look tired. They decided he would rest before dinner while Grant reviewed the mug shots from Pakistan.

Crystal changed out of her disguise, opting for a sleeveless blouse that molded snugly to her torso. She fitted a loose sweater over the revealing top that was a little more provocative than the FBI agents needed to see. A splash of perfume and fresh lipstick, she was ready to challenge the straight-speaking lead agent for female supremacy in the house.

Meyers was on her cell phone. "It's a match to the vehicle type?" she said into the mouthpiece, listened intently as a barely audible voice on the other end said something about being weighted down. "Do you have all the assets you need?"

"Yes," came clearly through the phone followed by a garbled rambling that Crystal could not make out.

"Right ... right ... Good luck." Meyers pushed end, turned to the group. "So, tire tracks in a bayou south of New Orleans match one of ours from the forest, maybe our guys." She eyed Crystal up and down, settling on her dusty-rose lips. "Tracks indicate a truck carrying a heavy load."

The meaning of that statement was not lost on any of them.

"Maybe the tip from your doctor friend will pay off," Meyers said. "They're heading in tonight, once they've got the entire area cordoned off." She looked at the young agent. "They've only got the one track going in. So unless they came out another way, they're still somewhere in that bayou."

"What about the Gulf ... could they be leaving by boat?" Crystal asked.

"Coast Guard has it sewed up like a purse," Meyers said, nodding ever so slightly. "They'll get 'em."

Who was the nod intended for? "Was the truck they identified the one my grandfather and I saw?"

"I didn't get that breakdown," The lead agent answered tight lipped. "We had at least two if not three tracks at various points along that road. Several more near the entrance off Highway 20."

"And maybe you'll get our good doctor before he's forced to complete his mission," Grant said as he pointed to the display screen. "Welcome to America, Doctor Amir Rashid ... Peshawar Medical Center."

"That's him?" Meyers said.

"I'm not one-hundred-percent sure but I'd bet a month's salary on it." Grant smiled at Crystal and put his thumb up.

"Good job." She stood behind him beaming and put her hands on his muscular shoulders. "Maybe this will all get sewn up before anyone else gets hurt."

Meyers' sidekick was already on his phone, quickly passing the demographics of Doctor Rashid on to the FBI counter-terrorism task force.

"We're headed back to the station after getting a bite," Meyers said. "To monitor the situation in Louisiana. Can we call you this evening, even if it's late?"

Grant glanced over his shoulder at Crystal and answered for them both, "Sure, absolutely! It would make for a much better night sleep if we knew they'd caught those bastards."

A flush rose in Crystal's neck and cheeks. She turned from the group and entered the master bedroom suite. Splashed cold water on her face and held a towel over it for a long moment. This might be her last night with Grant. It hit her like a kick to the stomach. What a mess, she'd fallen hard for the guy. Was there any hope of rescuing what they'd had the previous night? Could she beat her mother's curse?

The FBI was gone and Grant was busy in the kitchen when Crystal returned. "Hey, Agent Meyers said thanks for all your help, and your grandfather's."

Crystal smiled weakly, trying to look more with-it and enthused. "What are you up to?"

"Dinner. How's parmesan chicken and a nice wine sound? Kind of a pre-celebration."

"Sounds divine. You're not off the hook though ... the burial site cannot be desecrated."

Grant stepped back from the stove and raised a tomato paste covered spoon as a shield against her assault. "I'm sorry, Crystal. I've been meaning to ... you know —"

"I'm gonna look in on my grandpa," she said.

He tossed a towel against the row of cutlery knives and with a frown shook his head.

"You okay solo in the kitchen? I can get the table set or something."

"I'm okay by myself," he said, plunging the wooden spoon into the sauce pan and turning, hands on his hips. "Have been for many years now, doesn't mean I want it to stay that way."

She began to melt. He'd fallen for her too. That would make the break even harder. Why? Why did this always happen to Blackrock women? Whom had they offended so sorely? She smiled again in Grant's direction. This smile even weaker than the first. She was losing it, and fast.

She retreated into the guest bedroom. Her grandfather lay propped up on a pile of pillows, eyes wide open.

"Meyers thinks they may have found the traffickers," Crystal said.

"I heard."

"Grant's fixing some dinner," she said as she climbed onto the bed and lay with her head on his arm.

He gently smoothed her hair as she lay quietly.

Finally Crystal sighed deeply. "I do love him, Grandpa. But everywhere I turn I see a big 'Walk away, Crystal' sign." She buried her nose in his shoulder, hoping it would all go away, hoping that she would pull back and be that naïve fifteen-year-old, safe in her grandfather's arms.

"Did Grandma and I ever tell you life would be easy, fair, or safe?"

She shook her head and choked back tears.

"Do you think happiness depends on everything going right?"

She rolled to her side and peered up into the wrinkled face of knowledge and understanding. A face weathered by adversity, death, and overwhelming responsibility. "You're not gonna give me any answers, are you?"

"You have the answers, Granddaughter. You have always had the answers. You just need to find them." He took her head in both hands and kissed her hair. "May the spirits of our ancestors and the almighty Creator guide you in the Sacred Way." His arm rested on her shoulder.

Chapter 36

Sands' Townhome

Grant was beginning to understand. Crystal was struggling, certainly with their relationship, but also with a weighty responsibility to her people. He did not want to change her. She was amazing just as she was. But could he live with a woman whose daily existence was tied inexorably to an ancient past? Could they successfully merge her Creek culture with a twenty-first century family?

His grandfather had done it—married a full-blood Cherokee from the western Carolinas. Grant had spent many days at their farm near the Tennessee border, attended ceremonies and festivals. His grandfather had supported his grandmother's practice of the Cherokee traditions. They'd lived a mix of the two cultures, probably the better for it. Though his father had largely shirked his ancestry, Grant had made at least a reasonable effort to embrace his lineage and understand what being part Native American meant.

But his struggle was nothing like that of Crystal Blackrock's, born to the responsibility of carrying on the Creek healing art, and more. Her task was nothing short of joining the spirits of nature and her ancient kin in a way Grant could not fathom. She labored continually to mentally and physically bridge that gap. Any lifemate would need tremendous inner strength to support her in that journey. Was he capable of being that person?

In many ways, modern society was a distraction to people such as Crystal. A clear vision of the Creek existence was shrouded in consumerism, news reporting, and the chores of every day life. Grant had seen that, amplified by the effect of warfare. But Crystal's battle, to become one with the Sacred Way, would be every bit the struggle that the Afghan war had been for him. Was he up to the challenge? If she'd have him, he would work as tirelessly as his grandfather had. She was probably the channel he'd always sought to the understanding and acceptance of his native heritage. Not a painless path, but nothing worthwhile was.

Grant daydreamed of his night with Crystal as he aerated a bottle of Pinot Noir. For all of her petite frame, she fashioned a massive fire of passion and vitality. Expecting to dominate the wiry siren, he had instead been engulfed in her spiritual sensuality.

Inside the luscious and soft curves of this native maiden simmered a mysterious, magic, and mystical entity. In a different setting, he might have feared the influence of dark forces. He recognized it now for what it was. He loved Crystal Blackrock. She was his soul mate, his guide to a greater and grander existence and understanding of life. Of that he was convinced.

•

"To a successful apprehension." Grant raised a wine glass over his partially eaten dinner.

They had all eagerly attacked the steaming chicken and pasta. Crystal's earlier anger had simmered and as they sat sharing the warm meal and wine, the gnawing in her stomach eased. She was giving in too easily, becoming complacent. *Get it together!*

"To success." Crystal and her grandfather echoed as glasses touched. The wine was buoying up her resolve to address the burial site issue.

Grant set down his wine glass. "I'm sure you'll be happy to get back to the farm, if the threat of those traffickers can be eliminated."

"It would sure make keeping my job easier," Crystal said.

Her grandfather smiled. "Lots to get done, with the cattle too."

"Do you have someone to pitch in with the chores while you mend?" Grant asked.

"I have cousins and two nephews that can lend a hand."

Crystal scoffed. "They have jobs, Grandpa. And there is Uncle Tate's farm that needs fence work and the corn to be taken in. You're gonna need some help."

Her grandfather grimaced and nodded ever so slightly.

Grant put down his fork and finished chewing. "Well, I did

some work as a kid on my grandfather's farm in North Carolina. I don't know much about cattle, but I can follow directions. And I do know how to drive a tractor." He smiled at Crystal.

Was he inviting himself back into her life? Would she have to deal with this grave robber for weeks on end? Her neck flushed. Anger or the wine? Luckily, she had not said anything, yet. Don't jump to conclusions. She pushed away the wine glass.

"Looks like I'm not in a position to be picky," her grandfather said. He glanced sideways at Crystal as if daring her to enter the discussion.

Careful, don't say something you'll regret. "Hey, someone has to slop the hog pen, better them than me," she stammered. Yeah, a good time to keep her mouth shut.

"My leg won't keep me from helping you clean up these dishes," her grandfather said. "My granddaughter and I thank you for your hospitality."

Her grandfather was apologizing for her. The frontal attack on Grant should wait until her mind cleared a little.

The doorbell rang. Grant looked to Crystal, who turned to her grandfather.

"That's probably Micah," her grandfather said. "I talked to him last night. He said we could start setting up the cleansing ceremony."

Grant rose.

"Where at ... here?" Crystal asked.

"No, of course not. We need fresh running water. Micah agreed that the Econfina would be our best bet."

"So, what are you two doing tonight?" she asked.

"Micah's uncle has a place north of Highway 20 on the creek, said he'd run me out there to take a look. We might stay and howl at the stars a little too, if the leg holds out."

Crystal scowled. "You know you can't get that leg dirty or wet." She fought to remove the frown. "It's not out of the woods yet, Grandpa. It needs plenty of rest. You won't be ready for any ceremonial dancing or any of that for several weeks."

"I know, I know. You're as bad as your grandmother, young lady."

Grant returned with Micah Kanache as her grandfather made the introductions.

"I can get these dishes if you all need to hit the road," Grant offered.

"Nonsense," her grandfather said. "Pour Micah a glass of wine. He can chill from his day at the pipe yard. Right, Micah?"

"Maybe just one," the stocky Indian answered.

His face reminded Crystal of a weathered saddle.

Grant took a wine glass from a rack in the kitchen and poured it half-full of the pinot noir. "Is it a long ceremony?" He set the wine gently on the counter in front of Kanache.

Kanache swirled the wine and sniffed the bouquet, raised the glass and said, "To strength and purity."

They all drank.

Will placed a hand on Kanache's back. "The sweat only takes a day or so, but the fast is three to four days."

"Four days!" Grant said.

Crystal tipped her head toward her grandfather. "The time is spent preparing the chants and holy words for cleansing as well—"

"It's not just the organs that need cleansing," her grandfather said. "It is a total spiritual renewal. The mind and body, along with the words and singings must all go through a reawakening."

Crystal nodded. "The sweat is done on the third or fourth day after all the preparations have been completed. And then finally all the lost spirits are cleansed with fresh water … along with the chants and sacred words."

"I usually do it on the last day." Her grandfather walked stiff legged behind Crystal. His gnarled fingers dug deeply into her neck and shoulders. The tense and tested muscles slowly gave way to his onslaught. "That's the way Grandma Amelia did it."

Grant turned on the kitchen sink and began rinsing the pots and pans.

Chapter 37

While the boys cleaned up, Crystal snuck out the sliding door and around to the garage. She retrieved her roll from the truck and climbed the rise to the bluff. Stiff muscles in her neck gave in grudgingly to side stretching. Lush, thick-bladed grass beneath the moss-covered ancient oaks beckoned her invitingly. But a simple glance back to the house, to Grant, reignited the burning at the base of her skull.

Avoiding the occasional massive root, she laid the blanket in orientation to the paths of the sun, moon, and stars. Pushing and twisting the ceremonial poles finally took purchase in the hard-packed soil above the cliff. Spanish moss dipped low toward the ground and whispered poorly understood directions to her. Her shoulders relaxed

Seated facing the west, into the sunset, she once again lit a small fire of cedar chips and sage in the pottery bowl. The effect of the wine, though still present, was dissipating. Certainly many tribes used mind-altering substances to augment their connections with the spirits and Creator—mescaline, peyote. It had never been Crystal's practice. The effects of the alcohol would not help her journey, but it wouldn't hamper the process either.

The setting sun cast darkening shadows about the bluff. Gently a breeze presented a sampling of marsh air as a line of brown pelicans glided by on their way to an evening of rest. All was much as it had been on this sacred promontory for eons upon eons. Crystal's mind wandered as it frequently did during these sessions. Grant, a dead trafficker, the bones of her ancestors all battled in her mind. A deep ache pulled at her heart as she struggled to bring the happenings of the past days into harmony with her soul. This was the part she was not good at. So often she'd been unable to attain any reasonable alignment in her life, nature, and the Creator—but tonight she had to. She needed rigid focus for any progress to be made.

Tonight it was a lot about the cleansing. The ease with which Grant had talked of the Indian tribes along the Gulf coast baffled and perplexed her. Was it a hobby of his? Was he an amateur archeologist? He'd never really shown the hunger for knowledge and understanding that she felt. It was as if he were a spectator to the whole process of the Native American heritage. Maybe she was being too hard on him. He had been through a lot in the war. He'd seen firsthand the extremes of sacrifice people made to bring themselves into ancestral and religious harmony. This was passion of the heart, not something to be waded into haphazardly.

Grant was merely dabbing his toes in the pool of Native American history, getting a feel for the temperature, deciding if he wanted to take the plunge. But still, why? What drove him to seek meaning in her culture? He'd been hit squarely in the face with the Afghan culture. A society that sent young men and women to their deaths to perpetuate a lifestyle that was far from the democratic principles of America.

He did not understand the Muslim preoccupation with heaven and the afterlife. How could he appreciate the nuances of the Creek or any other Native American culture? Would he eventually try? Give himself to an experience completely foreign to his upbringing? Why would he?

Crystal readjusted herself on the blanket, moved the smoking bowl to the east, and faced away from the sunset. Stars laced the darkening sky. Mother moon had not yet made an appearance. It was a night of emptiness with great potential for discovery.

Grant's troubles were far from her mind, cleansed. But the musky aroma of his maleness and the coarse feel of his body against hers remained. Despite her efforts her loins ached—longed to feel him between her thighs—inside her, filling her. She fought hard to banish the thoughts, to center her meditation on nature and the spirit of her ancestors.

It was not working. Here in this most hallowed of locations, with the veracity of the Creek leaders and medicine people of the past at her very fingertips, and yet she could not push past her relationship with Grant.

Then realization welled up in the pit of her stomach. All these forces of her heritage, focused on this most sacred of bluffs, were propelling her toward Grant Sands. It was the will of her ancestors and the power of nature in concert. But why ... why would her duty at this time be to consort with a man, intent on dismantling this timeless ancestral site? It just didn't make sense.

Crystal rose in frustration and stomped about, inside the sanctity of her medicine poles. She stared into the blackness of the bay. Ran her hands through her hair and rubbed at the base of her neck, anything to get back in touch with this upside down revelation. What the hell was happening!

•

Grant sat in the darkness of the exterior garage wall. Will and his medicine friend had left. He watched as Crystal went through what appeared to be a disjointed ceremony or meditation sequence. He understood some of the Cherokee ceremonies he'd attended with his grandmother, but this was nothing like anything he'd seen before. She kind of looked possessed, stomping and pulling at her hair.

The warmth of the day was replaced with a pleasant nighttime coolness that lingered on his skin. Up on the bluff, beneath oaks draped in Spanish moss, Crystal's form became less and less distinct as dusk erased the landscape. Fleeting movements and facial expressions were revealed as the occasional flame from the bowl gave a glimpse of her sacred ceremony. He felt like a voyeur. Was he committing some transgression by loitering in the shadows?

She was on her feet now, pacing within the confines of her circle, or square, whatever they called it. Was she finished? She certainly was more active now. Initially she'd simply sat quietly for nearly a half hour. Now her head shook and she'd throw her hands into the air. Should he walk over and talk to her? He didn't think that was the right thing to do, interrupting her ceremony, but maybe she was finished. Maybe she needed consoling.

Chapter 38

Sacred Bluff

"Crystal?"

She stopped rubbing her neck and turned away from the Bay. "Grant … is that you?"

He stepped from the shadows. "Sorry to interrupt you. Are you okay?"

How long had he been watching? It didn't matter. He'd certainly been a part of the ceremony from the start. He may as well be here in person. "I'm fine. I was just finishing. Is Grandpa with you?"

"No, he and Mr. Kanache left a little while ago. I told him to prop his leg up on a few pillows when he got to the uncle's place."

Grant stood just at the crest of the bluff, the top buttons of his short-sleeved cotton shirt open and revealing the chest she'd meditated over. Her pulse beat like a drum in her temples and her stare lasted longer than intended, which predictably brought his next question.

"Are you sure you're okay? Can I help you with anything?"

Yes, what the hell is happening between us? She stepped off the finely decorated blanket and removed the medicine poles from the ground. She laid them next to each other and then placed the gourd, eagle feather, and bowl next to the poles. The pounding in her head eased.

She picked up the blanket and turned to Grant. "Care to sit for a minute?"

"That would be nice."

She folded the blanket twice lengthwise, turned, and walked closer to the edge of the bluff. The hairs on the back of her neck tingled as he sat next to her on the blanket. She avoided his eyes, instead looking out toward the calming blackness of the open water. Her shoulder muscles twitched and goosebumps rose on her arms and legs. Reflexively, she wrapped her arms about her chest.

Grant placed a warm arm around her and held her against his side. She sank into the comfort and security of his strength.

"Pretty dark without the moon," Grant said.

The faint rustle of water reeds wandered up from the base of the bluff.

"Do you believe in fate?" Crystal asked, still looking out to the Bay.

"Wow … that's a heavy question." He chewed his lip and then swallowed. "My grandmother did, but I'm not sure I understood exactly what she meant when she'd told me I was destined to do great things."

"Grandmothers are like that," Crystal said. "My grandmother was the one that initiated me into the healing path. She also told me I would be a great medicine woman."

"They neglected to tell us how difficult the paths would be." Grant chuckled and Crystal joined him.

"Why would you let the homeowner's association destroy the burial site and the sacred bluff?" There, she'd asked. Was this a chasm too wide for the two of them to bridge?

"Look, if I have anything to do with it, the site will never be destroyed."

"Moving it is just as good as destroying it in the minds of many of my people. The removal of remains, the desecration …" She turned her head and began to shake. "Have you applied for the permit to build the boat ramp?"

Grant reached to hold her to him but she pulled away and stood.

"No, I have not. And I have no intention to do so."

"But you're the head of the homeowner's committee?" Her facial muscles tightened into an accusatory scowl.

"Hold your horses," Grant said. "Your grandfather said you've been talking to Frank." He stood and reached for her hand. She let him. "Frank doesn't know what's going on. Sure, I'm the head of the committee, but I took it on to prevent the association from just bulldozing ahead on that lame project. Frank isn't even in the homeowner's association. He's been renting from me the last two years."

"So they're not gonna build a boat ramp?" The realization came like a slap on the back.

"Oh, they probably will, but not through here if I can stop them." Grant turned and walked back up the grassy bluff under one of the century-old oaks. He placed his hand on the massive trunk and pointed back down the rise to the cordoned-off burial site. "There was talk about a boat ramp even before I built the townhouse. It was during the survey that I found out about the burial grounds, I moved the whole townhouse complex to the west to stay away from the site."

"It's more than just a burial site." She walked to Grant and turned back to the bluff. She re-explained the sacred nature of the bluff, its strategic location regarding the path of the sun, and its historical significance to her people.

Grant again picked up Crystal's shaking hand and held it firmly. Beautiful pale blue eyes looked deep into her soul and caused her knees to weaken. "I will not let anything happen to this site or the bluff. Trust me on this, Crystal."

She did. She loved him and she was in his embrace before another thought entered her mind, held tightly by arms that would protect her through the unseen dangers of their future.

"My grandmother would never have forgiven me if I had anything to do with a reburial," Grant said. "I'd already spoken with her about what needed to be done for any Cherokee that might have been buried at the site."

"Your grandmother is Cherokee?" Crystal nearly fell back against the tree in surprise. "You never told me you were part Indian."

"You never asked."

Crystal was sure her mouth was moving back and forth like a fish out of water. "Your grandmother is still alive?"

"And well, at eighty-two years young. She lives in Murphy, North Carolina, not far from my parents."

"Is she a full-blooded Cherokee?"

"One-hundred percent and to this day an active member of her clan."

Crystal plopped down again on the blanket, unsure if her legs would support her. All this battling with the spirits, thinking a relationship with Grant would risk her children's ability to seek the Sacred Way, all along the light at the end of the tunnel just out of her focus.

Grant sat beside her. "Sorry for the confusion. I would've probably gotten around to telling you if it hadn't been for terrorists, traffickers, and my damn hang-ups about Afghanistan."

Crystal smiled widely and rubbed her hands in Grant's ruffled hair. "You've been driving me crazy, and Grandpa. He says open up, Crystal. Let the answers come to you." She shook her head. "Did you see me up here tonight trying to let the answers come to me from the great spirits?"

Grant smirked and raised an eyebrow.

"Did I look like a maniac talkin' to myself, a raving lunatic?"

"Let's just say it didn't look like any of the ceremonies my grandmother had taken me to."

She collapsed into his lap laughing. Tears ran down her cheeks. She rubbed her face against his shirt as he massaged the tightness out of her shoulders, tension releasing effortlessly. Arms around Grant, she melted into him, savoring the sanctuary.

He kissed her hair gently. "Did you find any answers?"

Crystal leaned back. She watched the firm, chiseled face that studied her. "It's beginning to come together, definitely coming together."

He beamed and circled a finger tenderly through her hair. "Does it include me?"

She pushed him back on the folded blanket and pinned him to the ground with her extended hand.

"What do I have to do to get an answer?" Grant asked.

"Maybe you need to do a little looking to the spirits yourself?" Crystal teased.

"Your spirits or my spirits?" he returned, licking his full lips as he focused on her mouth.

"They could be both our spirits. There are a lot of Creek/Cherokee families."

"Do you have Cherokee relatives?"

"On my dad's side, nothing we write home about." Crystal released her hold on Grant and rolled over onto the grass, looking up to the stars. "I never knew much about him."

"Was he from around here?" Grant asked.

"North Georgia, Coweta or something like that." Crystal grabbed a handful of grass and presented it to the spirits of the night sky. "He was down here doing some work with Fish and Game, I think. He didn't stick around long. My mother had that effect on men."

"I've been to ceremonies in North Georgia with my grandmother, it's been years though."

Grant brushed the grass from her outstretched hands and pulled her to her feet, pressed her close. Fluttering like butterflies began in her stomach and flowered outward with liquid warmth. His warm breath caressed the base of her neck.

"It would seem that we, actually, have a lot in common," he said. "And I plan to stick around for a long time." His hand slid softly inside the back of her blouse and his strong fingers stroked the tense muscles of her spine. Together they sensually swayed in rhythmic unity with the night.

Crystal touched her lips tentatively to Grant's. No fire or lightning bolts this time but a stirring that started fleetingly in her heart and blissfully worked its way to her throat and mouth. An incredibly delicate sensation that reached to her core, a feeling of acceptance that she'd never knew existed.

A whiff of lime from his aftershave teased her nostrils as the embrace intensified.

Hesitantly he pulled away, gently nibbling her lips. "Let me … let me get your things back into the truck for you," he stammered. "That's where you keep them, right?"

Crystal grudgingly opened her eyes, willing the moment not to end. She made no effort to move, laying her head on his shoulder and inhaling the rich essence.

Protectively he raised her face to his. "Come on into the house. There're enough emotions and sensitivities flying around right now, we don't need any extra help from our ancestral spirits to confound this anymore."

Crystal nodded, squeezed his hand, and stroked his neck with searching fingers. She spread the blanket as Grant retrieved the medicine poles and other healing effects. Once again, as she had on so many occasions over the years, Crystal lovingly rolled the sacred implements into a tight bundle secured with the braided ribbon her grandmother had given her.

Hand in hand they walked back to the townhouse.

•

Clearing the air with Crystal felt good. Yes, she was a little over-whelming. And anything worth her effort was done with vigor, veracity, and victorious intent. Nothing short was tolerated. Her grandmother had probably been the same as Grant's was.

Grant checked the garage and front door to make sure they were locked. He returned to Crystal, sitting at the counter. "I gave your grandfather a key. He said he didn't know how late he'd be."

Crystal rolled her eyes. "He is an adult and responsible for him-self. He'd better be anyway."

"Care for some Bailey's and coffee? I made it for after dinner. Before we all got involved in other activities." His mischievous glance revealed the overture was more than a peace offering.

Crystal slipped out of her sweater and arched her back. She twisted her neck to the left and pulled on her head from the oppo-site side, then did the same thing on the right. Grant affectionately rubbed the goose-bumps that jumped out on her bare arms. She smiled appreciatively. "Trying to anesthetize me?"

"Warm the soul more like it."

"You've already got a good start on that." She pointed to the display cases of arrow heads. "This all makes more sense ... I mean, I could always tell you weren't just into collecting for the money. There was an obvious passion there. But now the connection is very solid, magical even."

Grant sighed. She probably had a better feel now for why he labored in field after field. Searching for what ... artifacts, or mean-ing to his life?

He raised his cup in salute to the psychological insight of the woman and slid a second cup across to her. "I guess we're both searching for similar goals, just a slightly different path."

"To magical journeys." Crystal raised her cup and Grant care-fully touched his to hers.

"And to those we travel with."

Crystal stopped her cup midway to her mouth. Dark pupils mimicked the night sky. He felt her scrutiny, her question to him. *Is this what you want, Grant Sands, a Creek woman with issues to deal with and a long difficult life ahead?*

Then, she smiled with a sparkle in her eyes, raised her cup a bit higher, and took a respectful drink.

Chapter 39

Sand's Townhouse

"Penny for your thoughts," Grant asked as she studied the steam rising off her coffee.

"I'm not naïve to twenty-first-century America, Grant," she said, through knitted brows. "But I am bound to follow the trail set for me. Does it seem to you an inane journey into fantasy?" She breathed deeply and looked again down into her cup, as if her answer would come from there.

"Inane? Do you mean, do I think there is nothing to the healing arts of our ancestors?" He stood up straight. "You're serious ... "

Crystal drank from the cup, leaned back, and rested the warm ceramic between her breasts and waited.

"I'm sorry you had to ask the question." He reached across the counter, placed her coffee off to the side, and tenderly picked up her hands. "I am a doctor, trained in the academics of modern medicine, but I realize there is much more to man and existence than what is printed in textbooks and journals." He stared into their intertwined hands. "I search for more. I may never find it. But I'll keep trying."

"It won't be easy with the likes of me. You know that."

"I'm not asking for easy." He came around the counter and stepped between her legs as she sat on the bar stool. Casually his thighs rubbed against hers as he pulled her head to his shoulder and snuggled his chin in her hair.

The sweet warmth of his breath soothed her overactive mind. She played with the loops on his pants, nervously chewing her lower lip.

She sat still through several long slow breaths. "It doesn't all have to be difficult though."

He slowly butterfly kissed to the angle of her jaw, his fingers intimately cradling her neck. With a deep sigh, he scooped her up in his arms and carried her to his bedroom.

Under moonlight filtering through the bay windows, Grant pressed his body deliciously into hers. Tingling and shudders broke over her as she clutched him to her chest, the pounding of her pulse accentuating her need. Sweet lips attacked her with loving nibbles.

She wanted this man—all of him—body, and soul. This was her answer to the future. She knew it now as surely as she knew the Creator would always care for the earth. Call it destiny or call it fate. They would face the future as one.

The bed groaned, pillows flew as did pants, shirts, and underclothes. A button rattled across the floor. Now they were together as nature intended. Crystal reveled in the inexplicable peace the union brought to her.

Grant cradled her head and sensitively kissed about her ears, nose, and cheeks. He whispered, "You smell of dandelions in the spring, sweet and soothing to my lips. I can't get enough of you."

He shifted to his side and toyed with her hair as he gazed hungrily at her mouth.

"Hold me, Grant. Hold me tight so I know this is not a dream."

Hands pressed confidently into the small of her back. Flames seared into her core as their bodies melded into an ancient dance.

"You are beautiful, Crystal." Grant smoothed her windswept hair, buried his face in the nape of her neck and inhaled deeply. "I can smell sage and cedar. You truly are a spirit of the forest."

She fisted his hair with purpose and opened her mouth, letting out a series of moans and sobs as he came to her. Wave upon wave of fluidity broke over Crystal, melodic and repetitive. She never wanted the moment to end. "Grant," she whispered.

She clung to him as her mind spun in ever tightening circles, spiraling—exploding, and then collapsing time and again. Crystal glimpsed grand forests and woodlands where the Creator's creatures ran happily with reckless abandon—grazing serenely in plush green meadows—the beauty of nature lived to the fullest.

Grant stroked her face lovingly as the passions eased. He tenderly kissed her eyes and neck. Taut shoulder muscles relaxed to a softness against her cheek and the fragrant musk of Grant's maleness blanketed her. She held him tightly.

They slept in each other's arms again, neither moving. Later Crystal awoke and roused Grant with tender kisses. His breathing became fitful until he opened his eyes and passion enveloped them once again in the diminished light.

He lay studying her, brushed her hair with fingers that had experience more than most men could ever endure. She sensed his thoughts far away overseas, in another time.

"Time heals all wounds," she said.

"We'll see."

"A good woman doesn't hurt either," she added.

He smiled brightly. "Makes all the difference in the world." He pulled Crystal to him and kissed her shoulder, whispering in her ear, "I love you, Crystal Blackrock."

Crystal already knew, but he had to say it. Grant was not only declaring his love for her but his resolve to move on from the Afghanistan War and all the horrors it held for him. It allowed him to search out the meaning of his life with Crystal, and to plot with her their common destiny. A destiny that was written in the stars—of this, Crystal was certain.

Chapter 40

Country Club, Sands' Townhouse

Late that at night, Grant awoke on the foldout sofa to the bleep of his cell phone. Rolling out of the bed, he punched the retrieve button as a text message came up on the display.

"Call as soon as you can—there have been developments—Meyers."

Grant's stomach soured.

Crystal came out of the master suite dressed in the oversized shirt she'd worn to the court house. Her breast pushed against his arm as she leaned to read the message. "Oh, crap," she said.

Grant slipped on his pants, padded barefoot to the master bathroom and turned on the light. Crystal stood next to him.

He punched in the numbers from the text message and looked with concern at Crystal as the phone rang. He put his arm around her and held her close.

Meyers answered, "That you, Doc?"

"Yes," Grant said, trying to keep his voice low so as not to disturb Will.

"Forensics called me an hour ago. There was a third vehicle in the forest," she said.

"At the murder site?" Grant asked.

Crystal bent her head to listen.

Agent Meyers responded, "Not at the river but out near the access road, where they'd have entered the forest."

"What does this mean?" Grant asked.

"Well, the tire tracks suggest a late-model Chevy sedan, probably a full size," Meyers said.

The hairs at the base of Grant's neck tingled. "Do the Louisiana authorities know about that?"

"Yeah, they have scoured the area leading into Plaquemines Parish but have found nothing that's a good match."

"So, what do you think this all means?" Grant asked.

"Could be that local tie-in," Meyers said. "I just got off the radio with Deputy Cross and he says a Caprice Classic pulled into the Country Club area and drove toward your townhouse but then abruptly turned around and left. He said that was 'bout a half hour before I called."

Grant shifted his gaze to Crystal, who frowned back.

"Could be nothing," Meyers added. "Cross did say he only saw a driver, no one else in the car. It was a dark color but he really didn't see enough to say what color."

Grant leaned against the counter near the sinks, his back to the mirror, his pulse pounding in his temples. Crystal wrapped her arms around his chest and put her head on his shoulder, close to the cell phone. Their shadows played across the Jacuzzi tub and the frosted window above.

A small hole cracked in the window. The mirror shattered. Glass shards showered against Grant's back. He pulled Crystal into the bedroom.

Squeaking came from the discarded cell phone lying amongst scattered glass at the foot of the bed. Crystal scooped it up and answered the frantic questions spilling from the receiver. "They're here," she panted into the phone. "They just shot at us through a window in the back of the house."

"Stay under cover. We'll be there in fifteen minutes. I'm on the radio with Cross."

"They'll be here in fifteen minutes," she told Grant. "Cross should be quicker."

Grant turned with a small metal box and punched a combination into a series of five buttons on the top. He grabbed a pistol, slammed a sixteen-round clip of 9mm hollow-point personal defense rounds into the handle, and chambered the first round. Another clip slipped into his front pocket. "In my office is a safe. Combination is zero, two, zero, three, eight, three. There is a Ruger seven millimeter mag and a Glock forty caliber. Get your grandfather and get what you can handle. I'll work my way around back from the garage."

"Is he back?" she asked.

"Yeah, just after midnight," Grant answered.

"Where should we go?"

Grant crept toward the door to the family room and eased it open. "Probably make your way to the truck. Be ready to make a run for it." He squeezed her arm and nodded grimly. "You'll do fine." She'd done all right the night at Blue Springs.

Grant wished he had the .45 outside in his Jeep. The 9mm Smith and Wesson didn't have near the take-down power of the .45, but thirty hollow points was a heck of an equalizer. "We think there is only one, but don't make the mistake of assuming there are no more."

Crystal nodded. He turned back and kissed her fully on the lips. "Might want to get some pants on too."

◆

Grant moved stealthily along the floor of the family room, a barely perceptible shadow outlined by starlight from the bay windows.

Crystal literally jumped into her jeans. The increased law enforcement activity in Plaquemines Parish had probably alerted the traffickers that information was still coming out of Florida that could compromise them.

She mimicked Grant's slithering across the floor of the exposed family room. The hardwood scraped her knees. The door to the guest bedroom was unlocked, her grandfather still sleeping. She eased up to the bed and began shaking it. Luckily all the windows in this room faced the front, away from the attack, if there was only one attacker.

Flashing blue and white lights sliced though the window curtains and into the room. Deputy Cross. Her grandfather stirred and attempted to sit up.

Crystal pushed him back down and gazed into his wide-eyed expression. "Grandpa, there's a shooter out back."

Grant spoke slowly and distinctly from the dark kitchen area. "Once you have the guns, I'll move out back to cover you."

Crystal leaned close to her grandfather. "There are guns in his safe … In the next room."

He pointed to a door next to the closet. "There's a connecting door through the bathroom."

"Stay here. I'll be right back."

"How many?" her grandfather asked,

"Just the one ... we think."

On all fours, Crystal crawled through the bathroom and found the upright gun safe in Grant's study. The combination worked on the second try and she was back crouching next to her grandfather as an eerie silence settled in, interrupted only by the flash of light from Cross' car. Where were they? Was this the kind of terror Grant had suffered through in the fire fight outside Kandahar?

Again from the kitchen, Grant asked, "Did you get the guns?"

"Got 'em," Crystal said.

"All right," Grant said. "I'm going out back ... Get to the truck and get ready. Cross and I should be able to cover you."

"I can crawl," her grandfather said. "Give me the rifle."

She handed it over along with a box of shells. They each lay on the floor, loading their weapons. Crystal concentrated on the night. She intuitively perceived an evil presence near the water, near the dock. Under the dock! The shooter was under the dock. "He's under the dock, Grant!" Did he hear her?

A series of thumps hit the back of the house near the garage. Four distinct cracks followed from further away. Her heart slammed in her chest as she tuned in the direction of the impacts, listened, and then settled back trying to control her labored breaths. Grant was okay. She knew that. The assailant must be using a silencer.

Crystal retracted the slide of the Glock and with a metallic click chambered the first of nine rounds in her short clip. The distinctive sound of the bolt action on the Ruger followed. "Ready?"

"Ready," he said.

The leg must have hurt being dragged over the floor but her grandfather never made a sound. In the garage, they climbed in either side of the truck cab. Her grandfather rolled down the passenger's side widow and positioned the Ruger with the barrel pointed across the hood. The garage door opener by the door into the house shined mutely, that wouldn't work. She eased out of the truck and skirted around the bed to the corvette retrieving the remote opener.

Gunshots erupted from the bluff as Crystal climbed behind the wheel. Another series of thumps followed. They came from the area of the burial site or more toward the water. Her heartbeat and breathing remained stable.

"I think it's time to leave, Grandpa. He's clearly out back," Crystal said.

"What had Grant told you to do?"

"He said get in the truck but we might have to make a run for it."

"This may be our only opportunity," he said.

"Yeah, that firing might be Grant tryin' to lay down cover for us."

Another barrage of gunshots echoed from the bluff. Crystal hit the garage opener and waited the eternity it took for the door to completely open. Truck running, she hunched down behind the steering wheel and backed out quickly without squealing the tires. They accelerated down the street toward the fitness trail. Flashes of exploding gunfire burst from the elevated bluff. Not stationary but moving just beyond where the orange tape would be. A hollowness gripped her stomach. *Grant.*

She slammed on the brakes and slid sideways onto a grassy area next to the fitness trail. She bolted from the truck and crouched behind the hood, placing the engine between her and the shooter. Her grandfather repositioned himself at the driver's side window, Mag Ruger at the ready.

Cautiously she turned and surveyed the parking lot, the fitness trail, and the road leading into the subdivision. All clear. She turned and gave her grandfather a thumbs up. The spirits of long lost ancestors welled up in her. She suppressed a nearly overwhelming urge to holler out some wild attack cry that formed in her lungs and clambered for release.

Chapter 41

Bluff at the Country Club

Lights were on in Frank's townhouse but no one had come out. Grant silently prayed they'd keep put with their heads down. The floodlights to the east had been shot out by the assailant who was moving in that direction. Grant was out of position.

Crystal had gotten the message after his second round of cover fire and had slipped out of the garage. A few more minutes and the FBI would arrive.

Deputy Cross, pinned down at the back of the garage, would be in the best position to intercept the shooter when he came around the front of the townhouses. Thankfully, Cross had not mistakenly shot at Grant.

The shooter would probably move along the east side of Frank's townhouse. Grant cupped his hands and in a pronounced whisper tried to get Cross' attention, "He's moving around to the front of the house."

"Right," came a muffled low whisper from the shadow of the garage.

Grant hunched down and ran along the top of the bluff. Wind rustling from the west made it hard to hear anything from the front of the townhouses. His steps produced a soft crunching that would not travel far. The Blackrock truck sat silhouetted by a distant street light, sitting off the side of the road near where Deputy Cross had held vigil. A few more minutes ... they just needed a few more minutes.

Cross must have edged around the front of the garage. Before Grant could get in position, thumps and splinters erupted near the shadow that must be the deputy. The figure slumped but got off a couple of shots. Grant picked up his speed. The gun battle below would allow him some cover. He struggled to get an angle on the assailant and within range of the 9mm.

"Halt! Police! Drop your weapon!" Cross had rolled beneath Grant's Jeep. Bullets ricocheted off the metal hood as his shadowy figure rolled further under the Jeep's chassis.

•

Well, obviously that wasn't going to work. The dark-clad figure continued down the road toward Crystal and her grandfather. The silencer suppressed most of the fire from the automatic rifle, but a slight spark emanated through the darkness and formed a fleeting halo of gas around the bulbous end of the weapon. She'd shot pistols before. She didn't know what an accurate range was, but clearly he was still too far away. Where were Grant and the deputy? She worried about catching them in a cross fire.

The shooter paused. Then he angled away from the townhouse toward the truck and the fitness trail. Crystal felt the hard composite of the Glock handle. Despite the coolness of the night, her hands sweated and shook. She'd have to hold her breath when she shot. Even then she'd be far from accurate. Bracing the gun on the hood of the truck would keep it much steadier than she could ever do standing. These pistols with clips were semi-automatic. Every time she pulled the trigger the gun would fire until the clip was empty. She had eight, maybe nine shots. He'd have to be close for her to have a good chance of taking him down. Too late to get back in the truck and make another run for it. He'd be on them within seconds.

The end of the automatic rifle sparked repeatedly. Crystal ducked behind the hood. Paint chips peppered her. The repeated pounding of a sledge hammer rammed against the frame of the truck. A loud crack right next to her left ear made her grab the side of her head in pain. She turned away from the driver's door of the truck. A second explosion cracked just after the click of a rifle bolt. Grandpa.

•

Grant saw the assailant recoil as his shoulder blew apart. The automatic rifle flew in the air. The black-clad figure grabbed at his shoulder. A second bullet picked him up off his feet and slammed him to the ground near the side of the road. Where had that come from?

Grant looked back to the truck to see the barrel of a rifle retract from the passenger's window. He surveyed first the front of the townhouses and then back toward the bluff and dock. "It looks clear … I think he was the only one."

"We're okay!" Crystal yelled.

Cross' voice echoed weakly from under the Jeep, "I could use a hand."

Grant peered under the vehicle. The officer breathed in short bursts and held a bloodied hand over his lower left abdomen. No gushing blood. Hopefully no vital organs injured. From the front seat Grant grabbed a sweatshirt and pressed it into the deputy's abdomen. "Hold pressure. I need to make sure our man is down."

The shooter lay in an expanding pool of blood, not moving, the rifle a dozen feet away. Grant kicked the rifle further across the road and knelt beside the assailant. He wore a bulletproof vest. The second shot had been taken by the vest but the first had shattered the shoulder and continued into the thoracic cavity. The man was dead before he hit the ground.

Grant swung about defensively, bringing his gun to bear on Will Blackrock. "Christ, Will, you scared the hell out of me."

"Sorry, Crystal's over with the deputy. He gonna make it?"

"He wasn't bleeding badly," Grant said.

Sirens blared in the distance.

"You or Crystal?" Grant asked, pointing to the dead assailant.

"Me, she's a good shot but not in this kind of situation." Will ejected the spent shell and left the bolt open, flicked the safety on.

"A good shot."

"Yeah, I guess." He knelt next to the dead man, turned the assailants head to the side. "It's Nisar Tulun!" Will said.

Grant stared at the lifeless body. "Doctor Gabriel Tulun's son, Nick?"

"Right. Nick is what the kids called Nisar when they were growing up." Will said looking up to Grant. "He worked real estate with some of the tribe members … Crystal and I helped sometimes getting financing and all."

"And his dad has a tan 1500 Chevy Silverado," Grant said. "Drives a Mercedes most of the time but I've seen him on week-ends at the hospital with the truck."

"Yeah, you know I have seen Nisar drive it at times, and the Mercedes. White, right?"

"Exactly." Grant shook his head tight lipped. "This will tear Gabriel's and his family's hearts out ... I'm sorry it came to this."

"They're Muslim, the Tuluns," Will said.

"Yeah, they sure are ... Gabriel has been a real outspoken moderate though." Grant shook his head. "I don't know if this was a radicalization or just a financial thing."

Will exhaled slowly. "That's for the FBI to figure out, I guess." He handed the Ruger to Grant. "The kid probably didn't know he was going up against two veterans."

"You too?" Grant asked, his shoulders slumped.

"Korea." Will grimaced. "Their snipers wore vests too ... we'd wait until they raise their arms to shoot and then put one right through the shoulder into the chest."

Grant took a deep breath, closed his eyes, and nodded. They turned together and walked back to Deputy Cross and Crystal as the FBI arrived.

The bleeding from Deputy Cross' wound stopped with minimal pressure. It was unclear if Cross was actually shot in the stomach or had simply been hit by splinters from the side of the garage. Grant rode with him in the ambulance to the hospital where he would undergo exploratory surgery if needed.

Crystal followed in Grant's Jeep.

Outside the emergency department, Grant slipped into a shirt Crystal had grabbed from his laundry room before she bolted from the barrage of FBI questions.

"We have to quit doing this," she said to Grant, buttoning the shirt.

"What, putting on and taking off each other's clothes?" He smiled wearily.

"Men ... war or sex. Do you think of anything else?"

Grant lifted her in his arms. "Like babies you mean?"

She punched at his shoulders until he let her down. "I need a shower," she said. "And you're invited, after we clean up the glass."

He picked her up once again and gently settled her into the passenger's seat of the Jeep. Most of the way home he held her hand.

A silenced Nova's Discovering Pluto played on Grant's big-screen

KINDRED SPIRITS: THE HEALERS **185**

television as Will Blackrock, injured leg perched on a pillow, snored contently in an over-stuffed chair.

The shower was refreshing but both fell asleep practically before their heads hit the pillow. They slept in each other's arms—snuggling, satisfied and safe.

Chapter 42

Washington, D. C.

The sun crept through haze over Arlington Cemetery as a cooling fog drifted off the Potomac. Doctor Amir Rashid knelt on a woven woolen mat and bowed to the east, morning prayers. On this tenement balcony in suburban Washington he hid, virtually under the noses of the FBI. Via the internet, before dawn, he'd read the Associated Press report of the capture in Louisiana. They had acted decisively, quicker than he'd expected. His forehead on the mat accentuated the tightness across his shoulders. He would have to find another way back home when his mission was complete. But, getting out of America was not much of a problem.

He rose from the mat. A flash of brilliance illuminated rows of stark white marble headstones across the river—the light of a new day accentuating the sacrifices of American patriots, or the all encompassing fire of a nuclear holocaust reverberating across fields of fallen infidels. Was it a testimony to the past or a foreshadowing of the future? He knew what his fundamentalist Muslim operators expected of him. And, his family was counting on him.

•

The piercing aroma of fresh-brewed coffee filled the kitchen as Grant opened the bedroom door.

Will Blackrock sipped from a steaming cup as he folded back a section of the newspaper. He turned to Grant and nodded. "I guess this means the two of you are back on speaking terms."

"After a long heart searching discussion and one more life-and-death struggle," Grant said.

Crystal, clad in a large man's shirt and floppy scrub bottoms, stood next to him, her arm wrapped around his waist as if she needed it for support. "And a few other negotiations," she said, punching Grant's shoulder.

"Well, that's good," her grandfather said. "The great hope of the Creek Nation was not gonna get too far if she spent all her time searching." He reached into the cupboard and poured two cups of coffee for them.

Grant checked his text messages. "Cross did have a bullet in his colon, lost twelve inches, but he's stable on the intensive care unit."

Crystal sauntered barefoot to the counter and plopped herself on a chair. "I suppose nothing much happened in Louisiana, or Agent Meyers would have called. I am really ready for this to all end."

"Probably not," Grant replied. "She was sure up to her ass in alligators last night."

Will handed the cups across the counter. "Is it possible that you two came to some agreement on the burial site and bluff? We won't be seeing bulldozers over there today?"

Grant winced. He'd committed to Crystal to do everything in his power to prevent destruction of the sites. "I'm with both of you and I am willing to do whatever is possible to protect both the burial site and the bluff." He frowned. "Unfortunately, my tactics to date have been largely delaying the inevitable."

Will leaned back against the sink, holding his coffee cup in both hands. "You don't think we can stop them?"

"I have delayed any decision with surveys and anthropological evaluations from Florida State University," Grant said. "They wanted more time to get together the funding to adequately research the sites. That's why we are still here, three years down the pike."

Crystal ran her finger in a circle around the top of her cup. "They might recommend that the sites not be disturbed. The homeowners may have to leave it alone."

"Possibly," Grant said, "but in residential areas there is a precedent for excavating the acreage, placing the artifacts with the university museum, and then opening the area for development." He shrugged and shook his head. "Sometimes it takes years, but if the developers are persistent or if they hire legal representation ... nine times out of ten they'll win."

She glared at her grandfather. "Think, Grandpa! You've been in these battles before. What did you have to do?"

"If it gets to the courts, it becomes expensive and usually not good for the tribe." He rubbed his callused hand back and forth on his dry lips. "The tribal council does have some funds to fight such actions. But I'll tell you, where we have prevailed, it has been using honey not vinegar."

"What do you mean?" Crystal placed a bent finger under her chin.

"We have purchased sites if the developer could be convinced to give it up. Often they are pretty desirable properties, like the bluff. And that can get pricey."

Grant stood and walked to the sliding glass door. Wind buffeted the North Bay waters into occasional white caps. Turning from the door, he grinned.

•

Crystal asked. "What's on your mind?"

He waved his finger in the air and pointed out to the Bay. "Does the tribal council have enough funds to purchase my townhouses?"

"What would that do?" Will asked, looking from Grant to Crystal.

"My lot would be perfect for a community park and boat ramp. In fact, the site preparation costs would be way below that of the bluff and burial site."

"So, you're talking about a swap with the homeowner's association," Crystal said, sitting up a little straighter.

"A win-win for both parties," Grant said. "We can develop a park for the homeowners and a historical site donated to the Creek Nation."

"It could certainly work!" Will slapped Grant on the back.

"That only leaves one problem to be solved," Grant said, eyeing Crystal. "Where do I live?"

She turned to her grandfather smiling. "There is a lovely site for a home on Grandpa's farm, Cooper's ridge."

"Hey, what grandfather wouldn't want to bless the union of his beloved granddaughter with such a gift?" He winked at Grant. "You know … you can see the sun rise and set from that ridge line."

"Really," Grant said.

Crystal put her arms around her grandfather and hugged as the telephone rang.

Grant answered and mouthed to the two of them: "Agent Meyers." He listened and then asked, "What about Doctor Rashid?" He rolled his eyes at Crystal. "Thanks, and please let us know if anything else comes up."

"What's the word? Did they get them?" Crystal asked.

"They got the traffickers early this morning in a bayou near Jefferson Parish about fifty miles outside of New Orleans—same truck—three men, two Ecuadorians, one with a burned and scarred ear. There was a young girl with them also, heavily drugged." Grant drank deeply of the coffee. "The Tuluns have lawyered up."

Her grandfather nodded. "Looks like we're off the hook for protective custody."

"I would think so," Grant said. "But these guys are probably just a small part of that operation." He looked at Crystal. "They may want you to testify … That could be a whole other bed of snakes."

"We'll cross that bridge when we get to it," she said, patting her grandfather on the back.

"Yeah, I don't know how far Creek sixth-sense will go in a Court of Law," he added. "But if they were caught with a kidnap victim and in Louisiana … well, it might be a long time before Florida even sees those fellas, if ever."

"Right, and good old Doctor Amir Rashid has not been seen nor heard of. They've plastered his picture throughout the east coast and will be watching several of the mosques they think might have terrorist leanings." Grant massaged his temples. "I'll tell you, I have mixed feelings about that guy. I'm glad I don't live in his world."

Crystal hugged him from behind. "No, you don't live there anymore, soldier. You're in my world now, so straighten up." She kissed him on the neck and up behind the ear as her grandfather looked on smiling.

Chapter 43

Econfina Creek

Micah Kanache pulled back the deerskin flap. Steam rolled out and a refreshing gust of cool moist air exploded across Will's face and torso. Kanache leaned in and whispered in Will's ear, "The moon is up. Owls call to the spirits. The robes are at the creek whenever you're ready."

For the third time in as many hours Will stood on shaky legs. No food for nearly three days and the day long, unrelenting steam of the sweat lodge had sapped him to near exhaustion. That was good. The spirits of the dead, those not in harmony with nature, were more exhausted than Will's physical body. They would leave soon. This he knew.

"Drink," he said to Grant, handing him a ladle of dilute salt water. It wasn't like the old days when all they drank was creek water. Grant knew the composition of sweat and what electrolytes were needed for replacement, hence the "doctored" water. Actually, the mixture was a triathlete supplement. There was no rule against using modern science against unruly spirits of the dead.

"What did Micah say?" Crystal asked as she sipped from the ladle. The light robe clung to her skin like saturated moss, a minimal barrier against the onslaught of steam rising from the basket of rocks, fired stones they had repeatedly traded-out with Micah Kanache throughout the day.

"All is prepared," her grandfather said. Water drops fell intermittently from the goat-skin bladder that hung above the steam generator, sizzling each time one hit the superheated stones, evaporating on contact. "It is nearly time." Time to forsake the intense heat of the lodge and wash the unclean sweat and spirits from their bodies in the pure waters of the Econfina Creek.

Grant climbed off the high bench projecting to the top of the sweat lodge. It was Crystal's turn in the near scalding cloud of steam. He quickly dropped his arms out of the robe and tied the sleeves around his waist.

Will studied him but found no wavering in his resolve.

Crystal threw a towel on the bench and crawled up without hesitation. He couldn't be prouder of the two. They would carry the Creek Nation forward with strong and resolute character, with wisdom and compassion. He knew for certain that the future was unpredictable and fraught with dangers as well as opportunities. He and his ancestors could only give the young ones the tools and knowledge to adapt and deal with the world as it evolved.

"I feel much as I did when I came home from the war." He smiled at Grant. "When the spirits left back then they took a part of me with them, but they left a goodness and wholeness that has served me well for half a century."

Crystal reached down and took Grant's hand. They stared at each other. A look Will had seen long ago in the deep pools of his wife's eyes. Love certainly—but understanding, acceptance, and commitment.

He sat cross-legged next to the steam rocks. Closed his eyes and began the chant he had repeated numerous times in the past few days. He thanked the medicine men of old for their faithful adherence to the Sacred Way. He thanked the Creator for the blessings of medicine and his granddaughter. He asked to have all dark spirits washed from their bodies by sweat and the sacred waters. This he did with confidence in the ancient chants of his ancestors.

•

His grandmother had spoken of the sweat lodge and Grant had studied the practice. Unfortunately, what he'd never been able to grasp was the profound interconnection of mind, body, and multiple spirits that communicated, did battle, and ultimately found harmony within the haze of steam and heat. It wasn't what was typically written about, but it was the essence of the sweat lodge that every native healer understood.

"My grandmother pushed for this since I returned from Afghanistan." He sat on the floor for a respite from the intense environment, glancing at Will. "I wasn't ready to deal with the grip violent killing had on me."

Spasms attacked his stomach. He stretched his legs, prepared to roll on his side as the gnawing increased, as it had those nights in Afghanistan. Here in the sweat lodge though the spasm was nothing more than a tacit acknowledgement that death had occurred. That his only responsibility to the war dead and the men killed this past week was to give their spirits the opportunity for harmony. What they did with that opportunity was up to them.

He dipped the ladle and handed it up to Crystal. She poured it over her head and handed it back. "More?" he asked.

A mixture of sweat and water dripped off her supple chin as she nodded. "You've done great," she said through long calculated breaths. "I'm so glad we are doing this together. To me this is as important for us as marriage vows. We are committed to each other, to live lives untethered of worldly conflict as best we can. Certainly, we are only human. But we have to make the conscious effort every day to look beyond the here and now. Only that way can we truly prepare us and our children for the future."

His lungs filled with a quiver of contentment, anticipating the life they would have. Not an easy life for sure, but adventure and mystery around every corner. And always, there by his side would be his Native American Princess—counseling and supportive, loving and intuitive.

◆

It hurt to breath in the scorching steam. Of late she had taken to gulping the water as if she could never get enough. Her limit was close, but she would get through this. With the help of Grant and her grandfather she would rid herself of the spirits that bogged her down and sucked the potential away from her Creator-given gift —a calling that had to be recognized for her and the Creek Nation to survive the twenty-first century.

"Thank you, sweetheart." She slid off the bench into Grant's arms, fiery and welcoming. Over his shoulder she smiled at her grandfather who simply nodded.

"For what, the water?" Grant said.

"For being the wonderful man and grandson you are. For being on that forest path, and most of all for being ready to move on with your life … with me."

Grant pulled back and gazed with blue-eyed wonderment down at her. A tingle ran up her spine and exploded through her chest and abdomen. This was her man and she was his woman. That was what life was all about.

Epilogue

Blackrock Farm

Grant threw dusty gloves on the distressed wood table and slipped off his work boots, setting them next to Crystal's on the Blackrock porch. He was tired, but in a good way.

Crystal called from the interior of the ranch house, "Ed Hawthorn left a message, something about drainage for the foundation."

"At the house or back at the Country Club?" Grant said.

"The house, sorry."

"I'll get back to him in the morning," he said.

The screen door squeaked as Crystal stepped out, wiping her hands on a flowered apron that must have been her grandmother's. She hugged him, ignoring the dusty and sweaty shirt. "How's it coming?" she asked.

"Well, the lot is pretty well cleared. The construction team for the boat ramp starts next week. And, I talked to the surveyor and there should be at least a thirty foot buffer between the boat access and the burial site."

"The move going okay?"

"It'll be fine, Honey," he said, holding her at arm's length, and marveling at her beauty. Her belt was hitched up an extra notch since the cleansing ceremony Micah Kanache had done on the three of them. In three days he'd sweated off eight pounds and Crystal had shed six. He could use it. She just looked thin. But they were all doing well, healed from the gunshot wounds and moving ahead on the land swap with the Country Club Homeowners.

"The permits are only good for thirty days. I hope the weather holds out," she said, referring to the house-moving certificates necessary to move Grant's townhouse up to Cooper's Ridge. The prospect first seemed daunting until Will had mobilized his base of construction friends.

"No problem," had been the response from contractor after contractor. Ed Hawthorn considered it a challenge and a personal favor to Will. In the meantime, Grant was cooling his heels in the Blackrock guest bedroom and sucking down meals like a laborer. The foundation at Cooper's Ridge was pretty much ready to go. He'd done a lot of the ground preparation himself.

He slapped his hands against dust-covered pant legs. "I'll clean up for dinner, unless you have some work that needs to be taken care of first."

"Grandpa might need a hand unhooking the tractor. He's been out in the fields most of the day but came back just before you drove up."

Grant kissed her on the cheek gently before putting his boots back on and heading down the slope toward the rumble of the tractor.

•

Crystal removed her hand from Grant's shoulder as he turned. The setting sun blazed across her ring finger as the diamond of her engagement ring sent flashes of gold and orange racing after him. She sighed deeply and felt the edges of her mouth break into a contented smile.

"Don't you two be long ... dinner's almost ready and I don't want to have to reheat it. It ruins the cornbread." She retraced her steps into the kitchen and bent over the stove and stirred the swamp cabbage stew. Steam engulfed her in a concert of carrots, potatoes, and greens. Twenty minutes more. Enough time to check her schedule for the medical clinic in the morning.

The computer was still logged on from lunchtime when Grant had been checking e-mails. She refreshed and was about to log him off when she noticed a new, unopened, entry from APatel@yahoo.com.

Doctor Abdul Patel? Was this some kind of joke? Through the screen door she heard the tractor cough to a stop. The silence of the farm gripped her like an attacker. Was there something about Grant she didn't know? That the FBI didn't know? Why would a

Pakistani terrorist be communicating with Grant? If she opened the e-mail the computer would acknowledge the activity and Grant would know she had read the message.

She trusted him. He'd been there for her these past weeks in ways only her grandfather had ever been before. He had opened up about the war and had started attending a group with other veterans. But what could this e-mail mean?

Footsteps on the porch told her the men were about to clean up for dinner. A cool breeze off the wetlands blew through the screen door raising goosebumps on her bare arms. Fall was just around the corner.

"You've got about ten minutes," she called out to the porch, trying to keep a strain out of her voice.

"We'll wash up at the spigot and wait till after dinner to shower," her grandfather said. "If that's okay with you?"

"No boots in the house," she said.

Grant laughed.

"I'm not kidding, Buster," she said.

In a muffled tone she just caught the word "henpecked" from her grandfather.

"I heard that," she said.

"You hear everything," her grandfather said. "Even half the things I'm thinking."

The spigot around the side of the house ran for a few minutes and occasional laughs came from the two men. She met them on the porch. Neither of them limped as they climbed the stairs, both healing well. She kissed her grandfather on the cheek before wrapping her hands around Grant's arm. The screen door slapped closed behind her grandfather. She and Grant remained on the porch.

"I can't wait to be in our own home, our own bed," she said.

Grant looked toward the ridge line. "It will be a great place to raise kids. My best memories are of my grandparent's farm in North Carolina … I'd forgotten how happy I was in those days."

A tinge of the forlorn veteran colored Grant's face. Despite the recovery he'd made and would make, the horrors of the Afghan War and the plight of the Afghan people would always be a part of their lives.

"I want a bench swing on the back deck, where we can watch the kids and the sunset," she said. "And a barbecue."

The somber mood vanished. Grant turned with a smile. "All boys, I bet."

"Listen, if any man will need a daughter or two in their older age, it'll be you." Crystal poked an accusatory finger into his chest, grabbed his shirt by the collar, and led him through the screen door.

"You know your way around a tractor," her grandfather said, pulling a dirty handkerchief off his neck and tossing it toward the laundry room.

Grant held the door open for Crystal. "I suspect the soil here is a lot more forgiving than the rocky stuff we tilled on my grandparent's farm in North Carolina."

Crystal glanced at the computer. APatel still sat conspicuously at the top of the e-mail list.

The men went straight to the kitchen. Grant poured himself an ice tea. Chiseled forearm muscles stood solidly beneath tanned skin as he held the glass and drank.

Her grandfather raised the cooking ladle from the pot of stew, placed his nose near the heaping mass of venison, cabbage, beans, and assorted vegetables. He inhaled slowly. "Just like your grandma's."

Crystal swallowed hard. A dryness catching in her throat. How would Grant respond to the e-mail from Doctor Patel, if it was truly from him? Certainly this could be some sort of prank or setup from the FBI or Homeland Security, maybe Scott Lang?

"Have a seat. Quit getting dirt all over the kitchen," she said, slapping a dish towel at the two kitchen raiders.

Grant grabbed her hand and twisted it behind her back, pulling her firmly against him. Musky masculinity moved her as he lowered his mouth to hers and gently tasted her lower lip. Her breath left her lungs and a surrendering weakness replaced it.

Her grandfather coughed. "Looks like you two won't get that house moved up to Cooper's Ridge any too soon."

Crystal backed away, her face warm. "He's just being a brute," she said, wrestling herself out of Grant's grasp. "I'll dish the plates up, get your drinks and settle down."

Her grandfather turned to look out the front window, down to the old compound, as Grant gave Crystal a final teasing smile.

Shaking his head, Grant turned to the living room and the computer. "What is this?" Slowly he set his glass on the end table and leaned over the display.

Her grandfather turned from the window and pulled reading glasses from his pocket. He too leaned over the screen. Crystal put down the plate and stood at the entrance to the kitchen, observing.

"Patel?" her grandfather said. "Isn't that the terrorist guy that cornered you at the hospital?"

Grant had not touched the keyboard. With his hands on the back of the computer chair he turned first to Will and then to Crystal.

"I saw it a few minutes ago," she said. "Do you think it could really be from him?"

Grant stood upright and wiped a hand over his mouth and two-day growth of beard. "It's either him or someone from the investigation. No one else knows that name."

"Except the smugglers maybe," Crystal said.

"Yeah, they might." Grant stepped back hands on his hips. "And we don't know if the authorities in Louisiana got all of them … probably not."

"Are you going to open it?" Crystal asked.

"It could be a trick." Grant said. "Could have a virus or some sort of tracking program attached to it." He folded his arms and stepped back from the keyboard.

Crystal placed a hand on his shoulder. He frowned.

"You think we need to call the FBI or Homeland Security first?" her grandfather said.

Crystal and Grant continued to look at each other. Grant was thinking the same thing she was. His head shook ever so slightly. She smiled.

"No," Grant said. "They'd probably want to fly someone down from Washington to research the whole system before opening the message."

"And Doctor Patel, I mean Doctor Rashid, was straight with you that night at the hospital," Crystal said. "If it's him he's only doing this because it's important."

Grant nodded. "If we open the message, we'll need to be ready to leave immediately." He glanced at her grandfather. "If it has tracking technology, they may know where we are within a few seconds."

"And it could be the smugglers," her grandfather said.

"Exactly." Grant breathed deeply and sat down, still not touching the keyboard, folded his hands as if in prayer, and nibbled the tip of his thumb.

Crystal kneaded his shoulders. Tight knots resisted her deep massage.

"The way I see it, we kinda owe the guy," her grandfather said. "He did get the FBI back on the smuggler's trail."

"Where would we go?" Crystal asked.

"To the FBI office in town probably," Grant said. "But I'm sure Agent Meyers is back up in Atlanta by now."

"So if we open it, and think it's a trap, we get out of here and head to town," her grandfather said. "Just take what we can carry and skedaddle."

"Yeah, we have to be ready to move."

Her grandfather pushed his reading glasses up on his forehead. "Should I get the guns and ammo?"

"I guess," Grant said.

Crystal started through the kitchen cupboards, collecting Tupperware for the stew. "Grab a few changes of clothes too, Grandpa."

"Right, I'll throw something together also," Grant said.

Ten minutes later she stood behind Grant as her grandfather finished packing the Jeep. A tightness squeezed her throat as she fought down second thoughts.

"Okay, I think that'll do it," her grandfather said as the screen door closed behind him.

Grant once more looked at each of them. When no one lodged a complaint or sounded a warning, he advanced the cursor to the APatel e-mail and punched enter, maximizing the screen as they all read the terrorist's message:

Doctor Sands, I realize this message is unexpected. You will not be able to reach me or respond to the message as I will be gone soon. It is entirely possible that your local police or security forces have been compromised. I have heard from my handlers information regarding the trafficking operation that would only have been known by insiders. I tell you this because you can trust no one.

My mission will occur next weekend at the National Security

Agency in Fort Meade, Maryland. The bomb is small but contains strontium and cesium. The explosives will cause dispersion over a wide area of the compound. Many will die of radiation exposure, inhalation and ingestion. I do not wish this. But an explosion must happen. Emergency services must be activated and casualties need to be reported.

I pray you know how to make this come about and at the same time avoid innocent deaths. My life and that of my family are in your hands. Allah Akbar.

Grant studied the message, long enough to read it completely through twice.

Will silently removed his reading glasses and replaced them in the pocket of his cotton work shirt and shook his head.

Crystal pulled a chair next to Grant, resting her hands on his. "He's asking for your help?"

"Not before tying my hands though."

"Do you think he's right about there being a leak here?" she asked, knowing the answer—knowing that she was witnessing a strange alliance being formed between her scarred Afghan war veteran and a reluctant Far East terrorist.

"He's the one that has everything to lose," Grant said, pushing the chair back and turning to the window. He stared out over the cypress wetlands below the Blackrock ranch house.

"He's asking you to stage the explosion, the terrorist attack?" Will asked.

"Seems that way," Grant said. "It's a hell of a risk for him and his family though."

A twisting grip tore at Crystal's heart and then unexpectedly eased, being replaced by calm. In earlier times she would have interpret the feeling as an omen from her ancestors. Today she knew these gut-wrenchings were the inner battle of Grant's fears and resolve. Ghastly emotions they shared at the prospect of mass death, being replaced by a solemn realization that they were now foot soldiers in the battle against fanaticism, and it might be just the start.

"So, you don't think we should report this to Agent Meyers?" Crystal said. "What can we do on our own against terrorists up in Maryland?"

Grant sat rubbing his arm, tracing the outlines of his Special

Forces skull and crossbones tattoo, just below the motto Death before Dishonor. "I have some ideas," Grant said. "I'll need to reach some acquaintances of mine from the war though."

Crystal caught a glance from her grandfather. "Clearly, the next few months are going to be far from boring," she said.

•••

Rory Church

Rory Church is a writer of romance and inspirational fiction. He is a long-time Gulf Coast resident and member of Romance Writers of America. Rory is a Naval Academy graduate and military veteran. He lives and travels with his wife and high school sweetheart, who is the romantic soul and critical center of his writing. He continues to write overlooking the emerald waters of the Gulf of Mexico or while pondering the stream outside his cabin in the western North Carolina Mountains. He says, "Inspiration comes from many corners and the trail of life often leads to curves and drop-offs never expected. But it yields the pebbles and roots of which great stories are made."

You might also enjoy . . .

Special Forces operative Morgan Raush rarely speaks to the handsome, blue-eyed Russian agent, Dmitry Rurik, about anything except military business if she can help it. They've formed an uneasy alliance during their joint mission in remote Uzbekistan. But now, through a twist of fate, the two must depend on one another to survive rugged mountains, blizzards and enemy attacks.

In the midst of icy nights and glowing fires, Morgan discovers Dmitry is much more than she'd first thought—a man torn between two ideologies, a man driven by faith and family. Then again, maybe the spy is only telling her what he wants her to believe? Morgan has only five days left to sort out the conflict in her heart, and only five days left ... to make it home by Christmas.

When a truck crashes into the front doors of the emergency room, nurse Tracy Aspen looks from the eyes of her former flame to the body of his murdered neighbor. Little does she know the moment will become, quite literally, the final calm before the storm—when all her former military training will come back into play.

South Dakota Ranger-turned-rancher, Jake Moran, is trying to outrun a tragedy from his law enforcement days—a tragedy with memories he can't bury. Now the same Federal agents who turned his life into a living hell have returned, and with them, Homeland Security and the Secret Service. But why?